PANTHER'S CLAIM

Bitten Point #2

EVE LANGLAIS

eBook ISBN: 978-1-927459-89-8

Print ISBN: 978-1519509024

Ingram ISBN: 978-1-77384-008-6

Chapter 1

> **Mom:** Hey, baby girl, what did you do today?
>
> **Cynthia:** Oh, I just shot a guy full of tranquilizers, kidnapped him, and brought him to my motel room. He's currently duct taped to a chair, completely at my mercy.
>
> **Mom:** So can we expect you to bring your new beau to dinner next Sunday?

AND, no, Cynthia wasn't exaggerating. Now that she had reached the ripe old age of twenty-six, apparently her eggs were in dire need of fertilization.

"You're not getting any younger," said her mother.

"Time you popped some cubs and settled down with a nice boy. Have you met Henrietta's nephew?" That from her Aunt Sonya.

"I'll kill any man who dares think he's good enough for my baby girl." Growled by her father.

God but she loved that man. Bragging about her pops was something Cynthia had no problem with. A big man, a grizzly bear married to a she-wolf, he always did spoil her, driving her mother absolutely wild.

"She's got you wrapped around her little finger," her mother railed when he fed her ice cream just before dinner.

"Yup."

Unabashed at getting caught, which always made her mother smile. Mom might grumble, but she loved their close bond.

Mom would smile a heck of a lot more if I settled down.

Ever since Cynthia had turned twenty-five, one would think she'd crossed some kind of line that counted down the fact that she was wasting her most fertile years. Totally incorrect. Being a veterinarian and medically inclined meant Cynthia knew she had at least another ten-fifteen good years to squeeze out a kid or two, if she wanted.

If.

Right now, she just wanted to find out what the guy taped to the chair knew.

The guy she'd kidnapped.

Oh my God, I'm a felon now.

It proved more frightening and thrilling than expected.

Daryl—a name her victim provided after buying her a very blue cocktail—had proven a little more difficult to maneuver than expected. Huffing and puffing truly wasn't attractive—"Ladies don't sweat!" she could just hear her mother lamenting—but a little exertion and perspiration were unavoidable as she heaved his limp, and heavy, body from the car. Okay, less heaved than allowed gravity to help. Once she unbelted him from the passenger seat, where he snored after she'd drugged him hard, he'd more or less tumbled out of the car to the ground.

Thunk.

Oops. That might leave a mark.

A less-prepared woman would have had to drag his sweet ass—and, yes, her super villainous self noted his fine glutes—to the door. But Cynthia remembered something her dad taught her. *Work smart, not hard.* Smart was grabbing the foldable dolly and some bungee cords from her trunk. And, no, it wasn't strange she traveled with those.

As part of her job as a vet, she carried a whole bunch of things to make her life easier. She dealt with animals on a daily basis—the furry household, not the six-foot-something male kind. Given limp bodies were a pain to move—*mental note to self: next time I kidnap a guy, choose a lighter one*—a folding dolly with stretchy cords was a smart business expense. And what did you know? It wasn't just perfect for securing and carting around animals patients. It worked well with unconscious men, too.

I still can't believe I drugged him.

Then again, the plan was hastily hatched during the drive to Bitten Point. A good thing she had nefariously plotted given the second drink she shared with her target made it harder to remember why she should watch herself around the hunk. His voice charmed from his first uttered, "Hi, my name is Daryl." Given his practically irresistible charm, she was very glad she'd come prepared with needles strapped to the inside of each arm and hidden by her long sleeves. Still, she wondered if she would have the nerve to stick him with a needle and drug him.

And just how did a nice girl get the kind of drugs needed to take down a fairly large man?

Cynthia couldn't speak for all vets, but she carried around readied needles at all times.

Never know when I might need to tranq a rabid coon, or a seductive hunk.

She really needed to stop thinking of him that way. Attractive on the outside didn't mean he was hot on the inside.

But he sure seemed nice when we were chatting...and even nicer when we were dancing. His hips rubbing against her, his hands around her waist, his essence swirling around her in a heady mix.

Stop thinking that way. Daryl wasn't a nice man.

As she taped his hands, she hesitated to put a strip over his lips. She had no desire to silence him. Not with tape at any rate.

Kissing is much more effective.

And dangerous. So dangerous because with one kiss from those lips, she'd almost forgotten why she'd lured him out to her car.

Quick, don't think about what happened next.

Stick to the plan, she reminded herself as she wound the sticky stuff around his hands. To those who wondered at the duct tape, it should be noted she never left home without it. Duct tape would one day save the world. It certainly had saved her cheeks as a child when she used it to secure a quickly scribbled drawing to her wall, over another drawing *on* the wall.

A woman who believed in being prepared, Cynthia possessed a perfect storm of items in her trunk, items that begged her to go through with her plot to abduct.

Yanking on the handle of the dolly, she wheeled Daryl to the motel room door. Last one on the block, and since she could park out front, it gave her a decent chance of not being seen. Not something she'd actually planned, but a coincidence that now came in handy.

Fumbling her key before sliding it in and unlocking her door, she didn't waste time wheeling Daryl into the room quickly and then shutting the door.

She darted to the wide window gaping onto the parking lot and yanked the dusty curtains shut. Pitch black descended except for the red numbers on a clock.

Dammit.

I suck at this whole subterfuge thing. Parting the curtains for some of the outside ambient light, she located a lamp and clicked the switch. A feeble light illuminated the tawdry room. She darted back to the window and slammed the curtains shut again.

"Gunh."

At the sound, Cynthia's gaze darted over to Daryl. She'd strapped him upright to the dolly, and while his head lolled forward, she noticed the finger on his hand twitching.

He's waking again?

She couldn't help but curse. *Stupid, giant-bodied, very healthy, super healing, well-endowed... Oh, don't think about his endowment.* Hard to forget since she'd felt it press against her when they slow danced.

I can't believe he's waking up already. She fumbled in her purse for yet another needle of the tranquilizer. She was starting to run low.

How many is he going to take?

She'd already given him way more than she would have expected. *Good thing I had more than a few.*

The miscalculation wasn't entirely her fault. Shifters metabolized drugs so much faster than normal animals. "You're a strong kitty," she muttered, her lips clamped around the plastic lid for the needle. With a yank of her head, she uncapped it, jabbed at his shoulder, and pushed the plunger.

His body gave a twitch then relaxed again, but for how long?

Get him into position before he wakes up.

Heaving his dead weight into a chair proved interesting. It took more grunting and cursing and sweat than she liked. She might have wolf blood in her veins, but that didn't make her as strong as say a bear, and Daryl was one big pussycat. She just wasn't sure what kind. Growing up, she didn't meet many shifters, she and her parents kind of being outcasts and all—darn those closed-minded clans and packs. But not having a developed catalogue of shifter scents didn't mean she could mistake the distinct feline scent.

How he smells doesn't matter. It's his weight that I should worry about.

His heavy body couldn't curb her determination. She managed to get him on the damned chair—*Victory!*—and bungeed him around the waist before placing another around his ankles. But what of his hands, and the rest of him?

No way would those stretchy cords hold him.

The duct tape came to the rescue. What she didn't count on was using almost the entire roll.

Damn but he's big. His chest wide, his arms thick, his...

Focus. She made sure he was properly secured, ready for interrogation when he woke up, which would happen in the next ten to fifteen minutes given how quickly his body metabolized the drugs.

Shifters had a much more developed system for processing foreign agents, such as drugs or diseases, that entered their bloodstream. Their power for recuperation was remarkable. The way they could heal without a scar from all but the most grievous wounds was astonishing. Silver and fire were the only sure ways of truly hurting them. But only humans or the most depraved of shifters usually resorted to those kinds of torturous methods.

Speaking of torture...he was definitely at her mercy.

I could do anything I liked. Her body would have liked to rub a bit more against him, and her lips yearned for another taste.

The situation might not be the norm for Cynthia, but that didn't mean her lustier side didn't take note of the handsome fellow, and there was a lot to note.

She'd already dealt with his great size. She also knew that his bulk was muscle, not fat. Lean, nicely toned muscle that she couldn't help but feel as she lugged his unconscious butt around—*and when we danced. Remember how nice it felt to be snuggled in his arms?*

Yeah, she did, but she also remembered who he was. A possibly very bad kitty. A bad kitty who needed to give her some answers.

And this was the only way you could think of getting them?

Most people would have just asked. Cynthia had certainly meant to, but when she saw him sitting at the bar, her heart had skipped a beat. When he smiled at her, damned if her panties didn't get wet.

She couldn't say no to the drink. She answered all his flirty questions. Asked him flirty ones back. Yet Cynthia couldn't force the words out that she really needed an answer to. Couldn't bring herself to make that accusation.

Chance after chance arose to grill him—during their drink then that intimate dance, a slow grind that heightened all her senses. Every inch of her had tingled.

Under his erotic spell, she fell without a fight. The next thing she knew, they were in her car, making out. He kissed her, kissed her with a hungry passion she matched.

"Why don't we go somewhere?" he whispered in her ear as he nibbled the lobe.

And it was those words, those innocuous—or not—words that brought her back to reality.

Did he say those same words to Aria?

Cynthia palmed a syringe in each hand and timed it perfectly. In a double swoop, she stabbed him with the needles and released the tranquilizer. He recoiled, eyes wide with disbelief. Then anger. "Why you..."

The chemical cocktail she used was good. He never finished his sentence, and she implemented her quickly concocted plan.

Now, here they were. A first time kidnapper and her victim.

When he wakes up, he's not going to be happy. Nope, which was why she needed the gun.

Darn it, the gun. She'd left it out in the car.

Best she grab it. She might need its daunting presence to make the man talk.

Look at me, acting all gangster. Her mother would have a fit.

Chapter 2

Daryl's T-shirt of the day: *"When I'm good, I'm really good. When I'm bad, I'm better."*

AS OMENS WENT, finding himself bound to a chair, fully clothed, didn't bode well. Not that Daryl had anything against bondage. It should be noted that were he naked and with a lady friend, he would totally be *up* for it.

Alas, he wasn't being prepped for an erotic experience by a hottie in a latex suit. *So if I'm not tied up for sex, then why am I a prisoner?*

There was a light somewhere behind him, probably a lamp given it didn't come from overhead. It provided enough illumination to see his odd situation. He was seated in a straight-back, metal-framed chair with a plastic bucket to cradle his large frame. The kind of chair most often seen in cafeterias and, judging by the wobble when he swished his hips, not too solid.

That's method number one to escape.

Two was snapping the tape that bound him to the chair. A simple twist of his large upper body should do it.

Onto the third item, what of his hands? Those were, surprisingly enough, taped in front of him.

By who, fucking amateurs? Don't they know how dangerous I am?

Who the hell secured a deadly predator with their hands in their lap? It wasn't conceit to think of himself as perilous, just fact.

Daryl tested the tape binding his wrists together, only a few strips thick. Too easy, yet, he didn't break it right away. Never act too hasty, not if he wanted the element of surprise and more information. But he almost forgot his own rule when he noted the duct tape was patterned with...ducks?

What the heck?

He peered down and, sure enough, more of the happy yellow rubber duckies swam across his chest on the tape layered there.

Mmm... Duck. His feline did so enjoy a well-roasted one.

Apart from feeling a little peckish, Daryl was wondering if this was a joke. After all, this was the least intimidating abduction he'd ever heard of. When he recounted this story to his buds, he'd have to make sure he changed the ducks to sharks because at least they had big teeth. Or maybe he'd tell them he broke out of chains.

Yeah, big silver chains. That would impress his friends.

The dim light barely illuminated the place. Probably a good thing given he was pretty sure the pink carpet, worn smooth in spots, was a relic from the nineties while the television, in its hulking, plastic case should have collapsed the dresser.

A classy motel, probably on the side of the highway somewhere, used as a quick pit stop by truckers and those looking for a place to wash and rest on a journey to somewhere.

But how did I get here?

That was the question because last he recalled, he was chatting with that lovely cocoa-skinned woman—and he meant *woman,* with curves that fill his palms, luscious lips that would look perfect about waist height, and dark, curly hair that spilled over her shoulders.

Hair that I wanted to pull, which was why I asked her if she wanted to go somewhere quieter.

To his surprise, she'd readily agreed, and they'd gone outside. Whereupon she fucking stabbed him with a needle!

So wasn't it any wonder when she walked in, not even two seconds after his recollection, he blurted out, "You're the bitch that drugged me." And despite what she'd done, he still found her freaking hot, even if she did have a gun pointed at his face.

"There's no need for nasty names."

"Says the woman who drugged and kidnapped me."

"This is your fault. You left me no choice."

"No choice but to accost me?" How dare she attack him with her lips and sensual nature!

"What else could I do? You shouldn't have tried to get me drunk and force me to make out with you."

Forced? The pliant lips beneath his and the hot pants were anything but. "You could have said no."

"That's the problem. I couldn't, which is totally your fault and why I had to abduct you."

The logic went right over his head. He blinked. It still made no sense, especially the fact that she appeared irritated with him for being...too attractive? "I think this is the first time in my life I've been tempted to throttle a woman." And then kiss her.

The gun waved in the air. "You go ahead and try it, darlin'. But I warn you. I can feel my finger getting twitchy." She canted her head to the side and smiled as she threatened. Spoken with confidence, yet he caught how she licked her lower lip, and her breathing was a little fast.

"I have something to cure that twitch and a whole lot of other things." And, yes, he made sure she got what he meant with a wink.

What he didn't expect was that she would laugh and say, "You wish you were man enough to handle me."

A dare? How he loved a challenge, just like he enjoyed this repartee. If he'd found her appealing in the bar when they flirted, now she was downright scrumptious. "You probably shouldn't have said that."

Time to up the stakes and show her who truly was in control. He smiled as he snapped the tape holding his hands. Let his lips quirk as he stood, with the chair stuck to him, and flexed, sending it crashing to the floor.

She slowly backed away, the gun never wavering, a touch of fear finally sparking in her eyes, but not enough to worry him, not when he could sense her skin heating as well.

What game did she play? Was this a prank? Something concocted by his buddies? Did they wait nearby, ready to mock him for having been taken down by a woman?

He didn't really care.

Wanna play. And it wasn't just his inner kitty that thought it.

"I'll give you a five-second head start," he offered.

Because this cat did so love a chase.

Growrrr.

Instead of bolting, though, she pulled the trigger at almost point-blank range.

Chapter 3

Cynthia: So I shot a guy in the face.
Mom: Will he recover in time for
Sunday night dinner?

PROBABLY. She might not, on the other hand.

The look on Daryl's face when the paintball hit him in the forehead and then spattered? Incredulous, and funny, which was why she laughed.

As for his not-so-human roar? Yeah, that got him shot a second time, in the gut.

"Would you stop doing that?" he snapped.

The yellow paint running down his cheeks made his irritated expression more clownish than scary.

Since she'd apparently miscalculated—something

that didn't happen often, given she was good with numbers—she thought, *what the hell*. She shot him again.

An expression of disgust crossed his face. "Oh, now you're gonna get it."

Click. Click. The stupid thing jammed, and she was out of ideas.

Tossing the gun at him, Cynthia squeaked as she dove to the side. She wasn't quite sure where she thought she was going, but Daryl caught her easily enough and bound her tightly in his arms. They proved a lot more effective than her tape.

This situation probably wasn't good, so could her body stop tingling in excitement because he held her clamped to his chest?

But we like this chest. Her inner wolf liked it so much it thought she should lick Daryl and mark him as off-limits.

Um no. More because she did kind of worry that licking might lead to other things, fun things they'd probably both enjoy, if he didn't kill her first.

"Who are you, and what are you doing?" He gave her a slight shake.

Was he seriously trying to steal the whole give-me-answers scenario from her? "Oh, heck no, darlin'. This is my kidnapping, which means I'm in charge and I ask the questions."

Twisting her in his arms, he perused her.

She stared right back.

He fluttered sinfully long, dark lashes at her, which only served to give the paint clumping his lashes a chance to cling together. He squinted at her, and she bit her lip as she tried to hide her mirth and failed. She burst out laughing.

"This is not funny." Spat out through gritted teeth.

"Yeah it is. I mean, you should see yourself."

He scowled. "You did this to me, and I still don't know why. Why waste time with this pathetic excuse for a kidnapping? Is this some practical joke?"

"No joke." Not even close. "I told you. I need answers from you."

"So instead of asking me"—he waved a hand around the room—"you came up with this brilliant plan." He didn't bother to hide his mocking.

"I had to improvise." Had to because she'd not expected the level of attraction and confusion she'd encountered when she met him. Not expected the certainty that came from her gut, a gut that she trusted, claiming he was innocent. Yet, how could she believe he was not to blame when she'd not asked him a single thing?

And did I neglect to ask because I didn't want the answer?

Or didn't ask because she knew he wasn't the nefarious person she'd feared? And, no, she didn't fear. Hence why she'd gone through with her crazy plan, a plan doomed to failure because Daryl was right. She sucked at the whole kidnapping and intimidation shtick. *How did I ever think this would work?*

The problem of living mostly among humans and not shifters? Underestimating what they could do.

"Honey, you really screwed up."

She had. Still caught in his grip, she tensed. *Did I*

misread him? Is this where he turns into a raving lunatic and kills me? She wouldn't die without a fight. Now, if only she knew how to protect herself. Her mother said ladies fought their battles with words, and when that didn't work, Daddy stepped in.

Unfortunately, words seemed to be getting her in more trouble and Daddy wasn't here to save her. *Uh-oh.* Her breathing shortened as the extent of her error was made clear.

A frown creased his brow. "Are you seriously scared of me?" He set her away from him and crossed his arms. It did nothing to lessen his intimidation factor.

But Daddy did it better, and her mom had taught her that it wasn't size or strength that counted, but attitude. While Cynthia found herself still a touch scared, his attitude did somewhat reassure, and some of her confidence was restored.

She snorted "Scared, of you? Ha. You wish. More like cautious. Never know what you crazy feline types might do."

"Do?" Daryl arched a brow with clear incredulity. "Isn't that the whole pot calling a kettle something? I mean, let's take stock here. You committed at least three major crimes, maybe more, to talk to me, so I have to wonder, what exactly is it you're accusing me of being capable of?"

"You know."

"No, I don't, so you'd better tell me."

"Or you'll what?" she challenged, which probably wasn't the brightest thing she could have done, but her inner wolf still insisted they had nothing to fear.

Good kitty.

Which totally went against what she thought. *He's a bad kitty. Sexy kitty.* Trying-to-suck-her-under-his-spell-again kitty.

A sensual smile tugged his lips. "If you don't start telling me what this is about, I am going to put you over my knee and warm that sweet ass of yours with the palm of my hand. Naked."

She sucked in a breath. "You wouldn't."

"Try me." And then, as if to addle her further, he stripped off his shirt, revealing a torso thick with muscle, but also showing a few scars. Round ones.

Had someone shot him?

It should have made him seem scary—her mother warned her away from bad boys who ran with people who owned guns—but as he mopped his face with his shirt, wiping the paint clear, she couldn't help but stare at him, riveted.

The man proved more of a temptation than expensive Godiva chocolate. It made a girl want to clamp her lips tight and not give him what he wanted, so she could get what her body craved. Him touching her.

Sweet heaven. How good would that feel? But this so wasn't the right time and place. She just wished she didn't have to keep reminding herself.

Think of Aria. Aria was the reason Cynthia was doing this. Thoughts of Aria centered her.

"I'm looking for my friend."

He arched a brow. "And? That's not telling me much. What friend? Why? What makes you think I know them?"

"You know her."

"If you're that certain, then why not just ask me? Why go through with this?" He swept a hand at the chair and its flopping strands of tape. "Come on, honey. You're gonna have to give me more than that."

Why did those words sound so dirty when he said them?

"I'm looking for Aria."

Blank look.

"You know her. Petite"—Cynthia held up a hand to about her chin—"skinny girl. Short brown hair. Nice smile."

The more she spoke, the harder Daryl shook his head until he interrupted her with, "Honey, you're going to have to do better than that. I don't know any Aria. And you've described any number of girls I know. Why are you looking for her anyhow? Why can't you just call her? You're not planning to kidnap her, too, are you? Am I your practice run?"

The questions he tossed her way in rapid succession almost crossed her eyes. This wasn't going how it was supposed to.

Oops, I think I said that out loud.

"And how did you expect this to go?" Daryl flopped onto her bed and tucked his hands behind his head. She stared at him.

The devil smiled.

She wished she had her gun so she could shoot him in the crotch.

"I expected you to wake up properly frightened. Because you were my prisoner and I had a gun," she stated, still miffed he'd not taken her kidnapping and intimidation seriously.

"You had a gun with a red tip."

"And? What's the matter with that? It makes it easier for you to see that the barrel is pointed at you. You should have been scared."

He snickered. "I guess no one ever told you that a red tip means it's not a real gun."

Way to suck all the wind out of her sails. Her jaw snapped as she clamped her lips. No, she'd not known about the red-tip thing. Cynthia knew very little about guns in general, other than pulling the trigger seemed to work.

Which begged the question, how did she procure the gun in her trunk? Simple, she'd confiscated the toy from some boys who thought it was funny to shoot the squirrels in the park. She taught them otherwise with a harangue that would have reduced her mother to proud tears. "So you knew all along you weren't in danger?"

"Anyone using rubber duckie duct tape isn't someone to fear."

She couldn't help an annoyed mutter. "I knew I should have used the skull head one." But she was saving that particular roll for Halloween.

"I still don't get all the drama. Wouldn't it have been easier to ask me at the bar if I'd seen your friend?"

She squirmed. "Probably. But I kind of suffer from a syndrome. I get it from my mother."

"And what syndrome is that?"

"Acting without thinking. Usually on account I'm panicking."

"Do you always kidnap people and threaten them with death by rainbow paint when stressed?"

"You're my first."

"And last."

Was it her, or did those words emerge a little growly? "So did you see her?"

"I can't answer that if I don't know who this Aria girl is. Don't you have a picture? Something?"

As a matter of fact, she did. The last image Aria synced from her phone to her social media profile. Cynthia located it in the gallery on her phone and loaded it.

As she showed Daryl, she saw his expression turn from curiosity to surprise. "That's your friend?"

"Yes, that's Aria. She's missing, and according to this picture, you were the last person to see her alive."

Chapter 4

Daryl's permanent marker tattoo
on his arm in the tenth grade:
Mom inscribed in a heart.

AS DARYL STUDIED THE IMAGE, he couldn't deny
that was him in the pic, smiling brightly beside a cute girl
he vaguely recalled. When had he seen her—two nights,
maybe three, ago? She'd been a little tipsy at the bar, but
he couldn't resist her request to, "Take a pic so I can
totally make my friend jealous because you are so
her type."

Was this mocha honey the friend? And if so, was he
her type?

Why not ask? "I don't suppose you molested me
while I was all tied up?"

That out-of-the-blue query had her mouth hanging open, and she blinked. "Are you for real?"

"Totally. Want to touch me again and see?"

"No." Lie. He heard her suck in a breath before answering. "I'm beginning to wish I'd kept you asleep for longer."

"So you could touch me." He winked, wondering if it would drive her nuts.

It did.

"No," she snapped. "There will be no touching."

"But there already was. And kissing."

"Which won't be happening again," she said with her chin tilted stubbornly. Was it wrong that, amidst all this weird drama, he still wanted to taste those lips?

Where was the anger that she'd drugged and kidnapped him? Where was the indignation that she thought he'd done something to her friend?

Fuck it. She's cute. "Anyone ever tell you that you're hot when you're angry?"

Even hotter when she combined livid with aroused. "I really should have left you in the parking lot instead of lugging your fat butt inside."

Daryl frowned. "My ass is not fat."

"If you say so."

"I know so. And just so you know, even if you'd ditched me on the side of the road, I would have still come and found you."

"You wouldn't have found me."

"It wouldn't have mattered where you went. I still would have tracked you down." Funny how seriously he said that.

"Why?"

Because she's mine.

He ignored the determined thought. "Do you really have to ask why? To finish what we started, of course." Because he still hadn't forgotten the sweet taste of her lips.

He took a step forward, and she took one back, then another, until she had placed the bed between them.

She shook a finger at him, a finger he wanted to pounce and nibble. "There you go distracting me again, and you wonder why I drugged you. I'm beginning to think you don't want to answer about Aria. This picture says you know her, and I demand to know where she is now." The wagging finger stabbed the screen of her phone.

"Demand all you want. I didn't really know the girl. Like I said, she wanted her pic taken with me, but that was it. As soon as she had it, she was back partying with a group of people."

"Her last tweet said she was off to bed."

"And you thought she meant to bed with me?"

"Well, you were the last image she uploaded."

"I slept alone that night."

"Says you," she said, trying to cling to her suspicion.

He laughed. "Says my buddy who left with me."

"So you don't know where she is?" Her shoulders slumped, and he wanted to spring from the bed, gather her in his arms, and tell her not to worry.

Wait a second. What the hell just happened?

He didn't just think about promising aid; he did it. In a blink of an eye, he found himself hugging the crazy she-wolf and murmuring, "Don't you worry, honey. I'll help you."

"My name is Cynthia. But my friends call me Thea."

"Thea is a name for a good girl, not a seductive kidnapper," Daryl said, leaning back far enough that he could wipe the tears streaking her cheeks. "I think Cyn suits you better." Because he'd wager she was sinfully delicious. "And I want you to stop worrying, right now. We'll find your friend. I promise." He'd find this Aria chick and bring a smile to Cyn's lips and earn a juicy thank-you kiss.

And claim her, added his panther.

Uh no, we're not, was his reply.

We'll see, his cat taunted.

We're screwed. Yeah, they both thought it, but for different reasons. Me-fucking-ow.

Chapter 5

Mom: *Why didn't you answer your phone? I tried calling.*

Cynthia: *I know. I was ignoring it because I spent the night with a guy last night. (Pause.) Mom? Aren't you going to say something?*

Mom: *Sorry, baby girl, just updating your social media status to "in a relationship."*

SIGH. Perhaps Cynthia should specify that she'd spent the night with Daryl but didn't actually do the horizontal tango.

She still wasn't even sure how the whole sleepover thing had happened. Actually, she did.

It's his fault. Daryl insisted on remaining with her because, "There's two beds. Seems a waste of time for me to go home when I could just sleep here and make sure we get an early start on looking for your friend in the morning."

"What about your job?"

"It's the weekend, Cyn. You'll have me all to yourself."

Shiver. Did he have to make that sound so wicked? "Fine. Whatever. Just stick to your bed. No funny business."

"Would you like to tie me up again to make sure I behave?" He winked at the suggestion, a flirty act that, in turn, did wicked things to her body.

She told her treacherous libido to behave. Then she told her wolf to stop with her antics, too, since her inner lupine wouldn't shut up with the whole lick—or pee on—Daryl thing.

I am not urinating on him. For any reason. So what if her Aunt Noelle swore by it? There would be no marking of males, at least not today. Bondage, however... "The next time I tie you up, I'll be using chains. Great big ones."

"I like the fact you think there'll be a next time."

A rumbly growl poured from her, a mixture of exasperation and too much interest. How could she both want to throttle and kiss him at the same time?

Probably because getting close enough to throttle him means putting hands on him and having him in the right place for another one of his delicious kisses.

No more kisses. He would like it too much. She just hoped the whine her wolf let out wasn't also out loud.

Flicking the light off, she snuggled under her covers, back turned to him, her attempt to tune him out.

She heard fabric rustling then nothing.

"Do you always sleep in your clothes?" he asked, almost startling a scream from her.

"No. But then again, I don't usually sleep with virtual strangers."

"Strangers? After all we've already been through since meeting? I'm wounded, Cyn. What a low blow. Wanna kiss it better?"

Yes. "No."

Sigh. "A man can hope. And I was serious. You really shouldn't sleep in jeans or a bra. You'll chafe that sexy skin of yours."

"Skin isn't sexy."

"No, but the curves it's covering are. Would you prefer I said you were tasty?"

She'd prefer he *tasted* her. Ugh. Would her mind please stay out of the gutter? It hadn't been that long since her last boyfriend, and she had a fresh set of batteries at home in her rocket that kept her from getting too physically wound.

His concern with her clothes made her ask, "What are you wearing to bed?"

"If I said nothing, would that convince you to join me?"

No, but it certainly played havoc with her body. Heat flushed her skin as she tried to not think of him naked with the rough cotton sheets rubbing against his skin, his muscled body unfettered by any constraining fabric.

Could extreme sexual teasing make a girl lose her mind?

"Are you ignoring me?" he asked, derailing her thoughts.

"I'm trying to, but someone keeps yapping. Mind shutting up for a bit? I need to get some sleep so I can be clear-headed for tomorrow."

"Good plan. We wouldn't want you coming up with any more half-witted plans."

"I resent that." While her plan might have run into a few bumps, in the end it had proven fruitful. Cynthia knew more about Aria's last moments, and she now had an ally in her search. About time because the cops certainly hadn't proven useful.

The human deputy behind the desk at the cop station in Cynthia and Aria's hometown certainly wasn't interested in helping.

"You said it yourself. Your friend's on a road trip across the country. She probably lost her phone or is camping out somewhere where there's no signal."

"I'm telling you she's missing. We need to file a report."

"And I'm telling you that, until you have more evidence, there's no point."

The deputy wouldn't be budged, and Cynthia left the police station frustrated.

Wasn't the fact that Aria hadn't been seen or heard from since that fated image taken in the Bitten Pint bar enough? And what the heck was it with this town and its obsession with using bitten? Yes, the place was called Bitten Point and, yes, a lot of its residents were carnivores, hence the whole chomping thing proving apt, but still, just about every business played on that word.

Who cared about a town with no originality? Aria was missing, and no one was looking for her. No one was worried.

Am I wrong or overreacting? Could it be that Aria is just partying somewhere?

If it were anyone else, maybe, but Aria wasn't the type to not keep in touch. She and her bestie never went a day without talking, and it had now been at least three. Cynthia didn't care what the cop said. Her gut insisted something was wrong. Aria had encountered some sort of trouble, and Cynthia was going to find her. She just hadn't let her parents know. Mother would have forbidden it as too unladylike and dangerous, and Daddy would have locked her up and said he'd take a look. Which, bless him, he would, but Daddy was hobbled by a broken leg. A mishap at work that would keep him immobilized for days as it healed, then weeks as he fooled the humans who didn't know how quickly shifters could heal.

With no one else to turn to, Cynthia had to set out on a search. Anything for the best friend she'd met during her teen years when the wolf began to emerge and Cynthia realized her human friends would never fully understand her.

But Aria did. Aria came along in grade seven, wearing black, with several piercings in her ears and a tough exterior to protect a fragile heart.

Aria was a product of the foster system. Found abandoned in the woods at a young age, she'd come into her eagle younger than Cynthia, and with no one to guide her. But the day she transferred to the group home down the street, they'd met, mostly because Aria dove onto Cynthia, slammed her into a tree, and, with wild eyes, said, "You smell different. You're like me. Except more doggyish."

A rather rough introduction, but Cynthia and Aria, from that moment, became the best of friends. The very best, even after the group home spit Aria out into the world at eighteen. But Aria wasn't alone. She had Cynthia.

And now Cynthia had Daryl. Between the two of them, maybe they could find her friend, if Daryl was telling the truth. Did he truly have nothing to do with Aria's disappearance? Or had he done something to her friend?

The kitty is good, her wolf promised.

Yeah, but according to his wrecked T-shirt, when he's bad, he's even better.

And it was with that thought warming her that she fell into a restless sleep.

THE ATTACK, when it came, arrived on silent hinges, yet she still woke.

Uh-oh. In the excitement of shooting Daryl and everything else, she might have forgotten to lock the door.

Who cares? Move, howled the wolf in her head.

Trusting the instincts of her beast, Cynthia rolled and fell off the bed. She hit the floor with a thud and huddled as she tried to make sense of what had happened.

Someone is in the room.

Someone or something? The scent tickling her nose also had her wrinkling it. Ugh. *What is that nasty stench?* It seemed kind of familiar, like wet fur after a run in the rain, but with a strong mildew undertone mixed with rancid animal musk.

Whatever shared the room with her stank and wasn't here to play nice, or so she surmised from the sounds. Snarl, growl, and a heroically stated, "I've got this."

While Cynthia might have chosen to hit the floor for cover, Daryl went after the intruder.

Grunt. Thud. A muttered, "Stand still, you hairy fucker."

Such language! Then again, the situation might warrant it. With Daryl keeping the person or thing occupied, Cynthia dared to peek over the edge of her mattress wishing she wasn't such a wuss. But alas, while she might have an inner wolf, hers was perfectly content to stay on the lower rungs of pack hierarchy.

Fingers clutching the bedspread, she looked. Forget seeing anything in the pitch black. Only the red glow of the clock was visible, displaying the ungodly hour of four-thirty a.m.

The longer she stared in the direction of the tussle, the more she began to discern. Murky shadows coalesced into two shapes. One, naked but for a pair of briefs, the other... What the hell was that other thing? It stood like a man. It had the right number of limbs, and yet...there was something off about it.

Enemy. Her wolf snarled inside her head.

Well, duh, the weird dude was a bad guy, but what was he?

Since Daryl seemed to be having some luck keeping the intruder distracted, she scurried over her bed for the lamp, fingers fumbling for the switch and lighting the room.

Something let out a nasty snarl. Something with lots of hair, she noted, as she finally saw their nocturnal guest.

"Good grief, what is that?" she said, her voice low with repulsed wonder.

"It's a bad..." Daryl grunted as he struggled to get his arm around its neck. "Bad dog."

"Is it a shifter?" Albeit a kind she'd never seen. It seemed to possess many wolf characteristics, yet this hybrid shape wasn't something she'd ever heard her mother talk about. Animals didn't walk on two legs, for starters, or have such human eyes.

"Who cares what the hell it is? Give me a hand." Because despite Daryl's bulging muscles, he was straining to keep the slobbery jaws from snapping on anything vital.

"I don't know what to do!" Panic increased her heart rate. Pitter. Patter. Double time, and faster still, as the wolfman managed to turn them and slammed Daryl into the wall.

He let out a grunt. "Do anything! Zap it with one of your needles."

The sedatives, yes, good plan. Better than the one she

had that involved her whistling to snare the thing's attention, tossing a stick, and seeing if it would fetch. At least Daryl's plan might work. Hers lacked a stick.

Diving to the table, she riffled through her bag, spotting two more needles loaded with drugs. She grabbed them and flicked the caps off.

Holding them shoulder height, she couldn't help watching with wide eyes as Daryl and the wolfbeast wrestled for control.

When Daryl hit the wall again, she knew she had to act. With a shriek of, "Hello. My name is Cynthia Montego. You might have hurt my friend Aria. Prepare to sleep," she attacked, and by attack, she meant that she jabbed the creature in its hairy butt, which, not surprisingly, did not go over well.

It howled in fury, she squeaked like a purse-sized Yorkie, and Daryl snorted, "Did you seriously just parody *The Princess Bride?*"

"And now I'm channeling Jamie Lee Curtis from *Prom Night.*" Cynthia shrieked as the wolfman turned baleful eyes her way and swung hairy paws tipped in claws, narrowly missing her as she danced back.

"Oh no you don't. The only guy touching that sweet skin is me," Daryl—clad only in black briefs—snapped. He wrapped a thick forearm around the beast's head. He yanked it to him. "Drug it again. With the adrenaline he's got going, two ain't enough."

"I have no more," she cried, wringing her hands together. What to do? She still hadn't found a stick.

"Bonk it on the head."

Goodness but Daryl was good at thinking of logical

stuff under pressure. Grabbing the lamp, she ran at the monster, only to jolt as the cord didn't release right away. Once it did come whipping from behind the nightstand, it stung her in the buttocks.

Worse than that, though, the room was plunged into darkness. The pitch black didn't mean she couldn't hear them struggling and grunting.

But how could she aim if she couldn't see? A yank of fabric pulled the curtains open, letting in the feeble light from the flashing neon sign—Nap Bites.

It proved enough illumination for her to see, take aim, yell, "Hi-ya!" and bring down the lamp hard.

With a crack, the hairy intruder went limp. Daryl dumped him on the floor and wiped his bloody lower lip.

"That is one smelly fucking dog."

Cynthia might have taken more offense at his derogatory term if she hadn't agreed. Besides, he might be right.

"What are you doing?" Daryl asked. "Checking it for a name tag?"

Having dropped to her knees beside the hybrid creature, she could understand his curiosity. "I'm checking it out. Look at this. It's wearing a collar." A thick metal ring that hummed uncomfortably against her skin when she touched it with her fingertips. But that wasn't the only thing interesting about their sleeping intruder. "I don't know how it's possible, but I think this thing is part German Shepherd."

"Excuse me? I think I must have fucking misheard you."

She didn't immediately reply as she sniffed, gagged at the unwashed smell, then sifted the scents. "I'm not sure

how it happened, but I've treated enough German Shep-
herds"—because her uncle had helped her get the
contract with the local K9 units—"to say with certainty
that we are looking at a canine shifter, not a wolf one, and
in some kind of hybrid shape."

"It's a half shift," Daryl remarked. "Not easy to
achieve. And odd that it's holding even with it currently
unconscious. It takes a lot of concentration to hold
that shape."

Daryl was proving an interesting fount of
information.

"I didn't even know that was possible."

"Because not many can do it."

"What about the dog thing? Do you have many of
them living in Bitten Point?"

He shook his head. "This is the first time I've ever
encountered one."

"So he's not from around here?" Cynthia regarded
the slumped body and chewed at her lower lip. "I wonder
if he's somehow connected to Aria's disappearance."

Daryl never had a chance to answer because a
shadow blotted the light coming from the window. Before
Cynthia could turn her head to see, round two of chaos
erupted.

The glass shattered in a tinkling display of glinting
shards that sprayed into the room. Via the gaping hole, a
figure dove through, and it didn't seem to care or worry
that it might get cut by the lingering spikes of glass.

Then again, anyone with head-to-toe scales probably
wasn't that concerned about scratches.

Cynthia might have spent a moment longer than

necessary staring. Way more than six feet tall, possibly closer to eight, a two-legged dinoman spread leathery wings in their motel room and hissed.

"What is that?" she gasped.

"Whatever it is, I doubt it's friendly. Distract it for a second, would you, while I change."

It took her a second to realize he didn't mean clothes. While the previous fight hadn't left time to shapeshift, it seemed Daryl wanted something more than human fists to face the lizardman.

What of his request to distract it? She didn't have any live mice to dangle, just herself, a juicy chocolate morsel. Gulp.

"Here, lizard, lizard," she crooned. A forked tongue flicked in her direction. She recoiled with a disgusted, "Ew." Being a vet hadn't cured her of the dislike of being licked.

Although she might make an exception for Daryl, but only if they lived, which, given dinoman sported great big claws and bigger teeth, didn't seem likely.

Apparently, Daryl was determined to change those odds. A sleek black shape launched itself at the monster.

Only to find itself batted aside.

That pissed off the kitty. It yowled in challenge, but before Daryl could attack again, their first furry intruder woke up, and he was not a happy puppy.

With a snarl, he dove on Daryl, which left her alone to deal with the lizard. It turned a cold, dark gaze in her direction.

Eep.

She grabbed for something, anything, and tossed it.

The fluffy pillow hit the thing on the arm, and even she couldn't pretend to not see its disbelieving expression.

In full-blown panic, she grabbed another pillow and held it before her, an utterly useless shield. "Don't you take another step," she threatened, or else she might just pee her pants.

Think. There's got to be something I can do to avoid becoming this lizard's midnight snack.

She needed a better weapon. Or...

Her eyes alighted on her purse still on the table. It didn't have any more needles, but she did have some outside in her car.

Question was, could she make it and grab them in time?

No time like the present to find out.

The reptilian thing, tired of toying with her, lunged. She screamed as she dove out of its reach, her nimbleness coming in handy. She hit the table with her hip, but ignored that bruising pain as she dove for the still-open door.

At any moment, she expected claws to tear at her back, but instead, she heard a snarl. Daryl to the rescue.

What must he think with her looking like she fled? To a car that was locked. Oh shoot.

She banged on the trunk and let out a yell of frustration. A whisper of sound and a puff of air were all the warnings she had.

Move.

Throwing herself sideways, she made it out of the way of the wrestling pair, the four-legged panther of before now a two-legged beast able to grapple for domination.

What was going on? Two-legged dog men, a giant lizard with wings, and now Daryl, some kind of two-legged catman? Had she entered some surreal comic book adventure?

Bang.

The lizard thing was slammed into the trunk of her car. Then the roles were reversed, and Daryl hit it.

Off they rolled, to thud against the pavement, but Cynthia was more fascinated by her blind luck. In their struggle atop her car, they'd popped the trunk. She wasted no time diving in and grabbing what she needed. Shaking hands filled the biggest needle she owned. She didn't have time to fill a second because the dogman came bounding out of her hotel room with a vicious snarl.

"Good doggie?" she asked, pressing against her car.

Snarl.

"I've got treats."

A step forward with an evil glare.

"Fetch." She tossed the rubber cap to the needle, but its gaze never wavered. She trembled and held the syringe in front of her like a puny sword. While bigger than the last two she'd used, would she be able to use it in time to save herself?

The wolfman launched himself. She closed her eyes and...remained untouched.

Once again, a furry feline had slammed into the hairy impossibility and taken it to the ground.

Daryl had saved her again.

Or not.

From the shadows limped the big lizard thing, and it looked pissed.

Cynthia feinted left then right. It didn't fall for it, its intent gaze never moving from her.

She might have let out a whimper, but she remained still, watching it approach. Leathery fingers tipped in claws grabbed at her arm. They pierced skin, but so did she, the giant needle finding flesh. She depressed the plunger, shooting it full of drugs.

"Night night, gecko man," she slurred. Funny thing, she was the one getting tired. Sleepy. Eyes fluttering shut as she slumped to her knees and...

Chapter 6

Daryl's T-shirt: *"Poke me and die."*

WHEN CYN'S lashes fluttered and she opened her eyes, he made sure she saw him first thing. Not his best idea.

"Eeeeeeeeeek!"

He stuck a finger in his ear and wiggled it. "Must you shriek so loud?"

"Where am I? How did I get here?"

"You're in my apartment. I brought you here after the attack."

Far from reassuring her, his reply widened her eyes. "Oh no, did you drug me and then kidnap me? Did you take liberties with my person while I was sleeping?" Her gaze narrowed in suspicion.

"I didn't touch you." But not because he didn't want

to. Cyn posed quite the temptation, but he'd resisted. Barely. "Exactly what do you remember?"

She blinked as she nibbled her lower lip, an endearing habit he wanted to try—on her. He'd nibble that lower lip anytime.

"Last I remember, I was sticking the giant lizard with a needle. Did we win?" Her expression brightened with hope.

"Not exactly." To his shame, the sudden appearance of lights in other motel rooms, plus heads poking out, had sent the two creatures fleeing. One by air, the other on foot—er paw. Daryl could have probably at least tracked the one, however, sluggish from the narcotic in the lizard thing's claws, and not wanting to leave an unconscious Cyn alone, he'd opted to let his friends take up the chase.

While Wes, Constantine, and Caleb scoured the woods for the dogman, Daryl tucked Cynthia's luscious cocoa body in the car, out of harm and curiosity's way, and then dealt with the cops when they arrived.

It wasn't as if he could hide the broken window or the smears of blood on the pavement or in the motel room. Daryl stuck to the truth, and no, he didn't end up in a special hospital for people who claimed to see walking lizard men and dogs.

Instead, Pete, Bitten Point's sheriff, called in, on their secret frequency channel, all available personnel to track the assailants.

"What do you think they were after?" Pete asked.

"Damned if I know." But Daryl had to wonder, was the attack targeted? Were those two monsters after him or Cynthia? And more worrisome, would they try again?

Because of his reluctance to leave Cyn without defense and the fact that he still sought to stay ahead of the drugs in his system, he took her home, to his bed.

Was it wrong he admired how good she looked against his royal blue sheets? He managed to remain a gentleman—albeit reluctantly. He left her dressed, and untouched. While he did think of binding her, with silk scarves to his bedposts, he didn't. Why resort to props when he could hold her down himself?

"What are you doing on top of me?" she asked, quite breathless.

Pulling her arms over her head, he pinned them so she couldn't fight. "I am making sure you don't go anywhere."

"I was just trying to sit up."

Why? He liked her flat on her back, with him pressing against her. "Why were those things after you?"

"Me?" Either she didn't know, or she had some kick-ass acting skills. "Who says it wasn't just a random attack?"

His gut did. "I think you were targeted."

"But why? And for what? Do you think this has to do with Aria?"

Did it? Either those things were after Cynthia because she was poking around, asking about her friend, or the disappearances were happening again.

Was Aria a victim? Had Cynthia almost become one, too?

If I'd not decided to spend the night to drive her nuts, she would have gone missing, too, I'll bet. Missing or dead?

Either possibility blew. And it wasn't that he suddenly cared about Cynthia or anything. Nope. The woman was just a curiosity, something his cat wanted to check out.

Naked.

Then mark.

Permanently.

Uh, no.

Daryl shook his head, meaning to chastise his inner feline, but Cynthia caught the gesture.

"Why does it look like you're arguing with yourself?"

"What would make you think that?" he asked.

"Because I often argue with my wolf, too." She smiled, an impish and, at the same time, sheepish grin that hit him below the belt, and she noticed. Her eyes widened.

Before she could remark on his rather impressive hard-on—because his girth made it difficult to miss—fact, not arrogance—he asked quickly, "Why the hell didn't you shift into your wolf during the fight? It would have probably been better than the pillow you used as a deadly missile."

He didn't miss the heat suddenly flushing her cheeks. "Um, my Lycan side doesn't like to come out in front of strangers."

"We were in a life-and-death situation. Surely she could have made an exception."

"No, and I don't know why you're making a big deal about it, seeing as how we prevailed."

"Barely."

"Is that why you drugged me? Because you were mad?"

He leaned forward until their noses touched. "I did not drug you. The lizard thing did, but given you're awake, it seems the effect is wearing off."

"Then why do I feel so lethargic?"

Should he explain it wasn't lethargy but smoldering interest that stole her strength? "That's not the drugs, Cyn. That's all me." He smiled, a slow, sensual curve of his lips. "I'm game to stay in bed if you are."

"We can't."

"Why not?"

"Because we don't even know each other."

"Hi, my name is Daryl, and I think you're fucking crazy, but hot." More than hot, she totally made his inner kitty wish it could purr.

"You should get off me."

"No."

"What do you mean no?" She pulled at the hands tethering her, and she bucked under the weight of his body, not that either dislodged him.

"That's it, honey. Keep squirming. That feels *good.*" He showed her how good and ground his hips against her.

"Oh." She gasped, but before she could say more, his lips slanted across hers with a firm claim.

He'd wondered, in the time since their last kiss, if perhaps alcohol or something else had turned their first embrace into something more. How could an almost stranger ignite his blood and have him throbbing so quickly and so hard?

He wasn't drunk now.

He couldn't blame the drugs.

Touching her lips proved even more electric than the first time, the taste of her exquisite, the feel of her under him...dangerous.

Dangerous because it made him forget he needed answers.

I think I might understand why she felt the need to act so rash. She wasn't the only one who couldn't stay focused.

Rolling off her, he tried to ignore her soft sigh of loss. *I wish we had more time to play, too, honey.*

"I'm going to need to know everything you can tell me about your friend," he said, his back turned to her lest he lose control once more.

Don't mock his lack of restraint. It had happened once already when he'd stepped back to admire her on his bed then found himself covering her as soon as she twitched a muscle.

"What do you want to know?"

"Everything." It took about fifteen minutes for him to fish all the relevant info from Cynthia, such as Aria's appearance, itinerary, all the images she'd posted before her disappearance, and the facts that Cyn liked to gesticulate with her hands as she spoke and she had the most delightful lips.

"...and that's how I ended up at Bitten Pint bar last night looking for you."

He interrupted her. "Do you have a boyfriend?"

"No, and neither did Aria. I highly doubt it's her ex

trying to get back with her. He's moved on with some other chick. Last I heard they were getting married."

"So no special someone back home?" And no, he couldn't believe he asked either. Shoot him now.

"Nope, Aria is single."

"I was asking about you. Do you have anyone special back home?"

"No, and I don't know why you're asking. I'm not the one missing."

"A man likes to know if a woman is spoken for before he makes a play. I'd hate to have to hurt someone."

He was really starting to enjoy the way he could startle her. Now if only she wouldn't keep startling him back.

"Well, given you've already made a few moves, I'd say it's kind of late to ask. Just like it's probably a little too late to tell you that I have jealousy issues. So, since you seem intent on trying to seduce me, I should warn you. I don't share."

"I thought sharing was caring."

"That goes for desserts, not boyfriends."

"I didn't realize we'd jumped from me putting the moves on you to us dating."

"We aren't dating."

He smirked. "And yet we've already spent the night together."

"Because you promised to help me find Aria. I don't even think you're my type."

"Got a thing against Latino men?" It wouldn't be the first time he encountered some unwarranted hostility.

"No, I have a thing against guys who are too hot for their own good."

He couldn't help a surge of warmth. "You think I'm hot?"

"No." A blatant lie given the blush and heat radiating from her body.

"I think you're hot, too." Even if her hair was a fluffy halo around her head. She'd lost the elastic that held it back. He hoped she never found it again because she was damned cute.

And that's a nice handful for pulling.
Rowr.

"I know I'm hot." She rolled her eyes as if it was obvious, and he laughed. "But hands off, Casanova. I am here on serious business."

"So does this mean no hooking up?"

She snorted. "Will you stop trying if I say no?"

"No." Said with an unrepentant grin.

"Then expect to get shot down. Now, if you can direct a bit of blood from your groin to your head, can we get back to finding Aria?"

A knock at his apartment door saved him from the fabulous insanity that was Cyn. He left the bedroom and headed to the door. He didn't need to peek to know who was there. He flung open the portal to find Constantine and Wes standing on the stoop. A peek behind them showed no one else. "Where's Caleb?" Daryl asked.

"Gone home to check on Renny and his kid. If there's another lizard thing running—"

"—flying."

"—around, then we'll need to be vigilant."

"You mean you've seen that thing before?" said the woman he should have tied to the bed.

Cynthia, thankfully dressed, despite his best attempts to get her to shed clothes at bedtime, appeared by his side.

What possessed him to curl a possessive arm around her waist?

It didn't go unnoted.

"Is this the chick those things were after?" Wes asked with an arch of his brow.

"This chick is called Cynthia," she remarked, but at the same time, she didn't move away from his loose embrace.

A bite of Daryl's tongue prevented him from saying, *Mine.*

Cyn didn't belong to him. And she never would. Daryl must really need to get some sleep, or those drugs were still affecting him, because his inner feline was acting awfully weird. Daryl wasn't into anything long term or serious, even if Cyn was a babe.

Seeing a girl a few times, no strings, that was cool. Anything that involved a toothbrush in his bathroom, half his closet gone, and boxes of feminine unmentionables in his hall closet? Never. Not happening.

He'd grown up with a mom and sister. He loved them both, but damn, those crazy women drove him mental.

What idiot would volunteer for that? No sex was that good.

It seemed extreme, and while he didn't mind trying his hand at many a daring sport, the whole relationship thing wasn't his scene.

And I usually move on when a girl shoots me down.
Not to mention, he shouldn't even like Cyn, especially
considering what she'd done. Drugged a guy. *Made out
with me.* Kidnapped him. *Put her hands all over my body.*
Restrained him. *Bondage!* Shot him. *Which so deserved a
spanking.* His hand on her—

"Dude! Pay attention." Constantine snapped his
fingers in front of him.

"What?" Daryl asked.

"What should we do next since we didn't find
anything? The freaking trail stops by the main road, not
even a half-click from the motel. Looks like someone gave
our thing a ride."

"A monster with a human buddy?" A crease pulled at
Daryl's brow.

"The thing did wear a collar," Cyn added. "And it
had this odd buzzy feeling to it. Could someone be
controlling it?"

"Even better question, what is it?" Wes leaned
against the wall, jeaned leg bent, his boots unlaced and
scuffed. The T-shirt he wore rivaled Daryl's with its
vintage KISS logo. "I ain't never smelled anything like
them before. And everyone else I've talked to says
the same."

Cyn waved her hands. "One of them is part canine.
How does that happen? Is it a shifter or something
else?"

"You mean like the Sasquatch in Canada?" Those
big, hairy things were big, hairy things. They didn't magi-
cally shrink into humans that could easily hide. Instead,
they lived scattered on plots of land that spanned acres.

People might mock Bigfoots, but they were really fun to drink with.

Shaking his head, Constantine tapped his nose. "I don't think they're proper shifters. They don't smell right."

"They do have a certain alien quality, and their ability to hold that hybrid shape means that might be their natural form."

"So calling it dogman and dinoman is accurate?" Wes snorted. "Can't we change it to something a little less cartoonish sounding?"

"It is what it is," Constantine said.

"At least now we've got a little more evidence than before. Blood samples were taken from the scene and sent to Bittech for analysis."

"When will we get the results?" Daryl asked.

Wes shrugged. "We'll start getting data in a few hours, but the full battery will take a few days to process. In the meantime, I think enough people saw something tonight that we can maybe stir some shit up about it."

"You're not afraid someone will go missing again?"

The last time one of their group had tried to call a town meeting with their suspicions that there was something wrong in Bitten Point, that person had disappeared. Wes said he'd given up hope on finding his missing brother, yet Daryl knew Wes still looked, every free moment he had, convinced his sibling was out there somewhere in the bayou.

It happened every so often that a person morphed into their animal and didn't come back. Ever. Those shifters were called wildlings. A cute name to describe a horrible state that meant the animal took over and the human part of the mind was trapped. It mostly happened among the emotionally wounded. But had Wes's brother, Brandon, gone wild, or had something more nefarious happened? Something related to that dinoman and furball?

When his buddies left, promising to catch up again in the morning, Daryl locked the door and turned to Cyn.

"We should go to bed." Daryl let his lips quirk as he said it.

Cyn backed away from him. "No thanks. I'm wide awake. We should start looking."

Shaking his head, he shot down her idea. "It's after one in the morning."

Her brows shot high. "How is that possible? Those monsters attacked us at like four a.m."

"They did, and then you napped the day away. We both did." He locked all the doors and finally collapsed. "At this point, dawn is only a few hours away. Businesses we need to visit are closed. Exactly where will you look?"

Now some women might have proven stubborn at this point and continued to refute simple logic. Man logic. The right kind of logic.

A logic she grasped?

"You're right." She smiled and stretched, back arching, breasts thrusting forward. "We should go to bed." She turned and presented that sweet booty of hers. An ass a man could totally sink his teeth into.

And he would. He caught up to her and reached to grab Cyn, except she scooted out of the way.

"What do you think you're doing, kitty-cat?" She tossed him a look over her shoulder.

"Kitty-cat? That's not exactly a very masculine name. Couldn't we go with something else?"

"Prefer Casanova, do you?"

He froze and frowned. "No."

"I like Kitty-cat. It's cute."

Usually, being called cute would work for him, but he got the impression she didn't mean it in the most complimentary way. Why would she insult him? The realization made him smile. "I see the game you're playing." Hard to get.

"Good." She turned, framed in the doorway to the bedroom. "We can play some more in the morning. Night."

When she would have shut the door—with him on the outside!—he interjected his foot. "What are you doing?"

She peeked through the crack, eyes dancing with mirth, lips a sensual smile of teasing. "I am going to bed. In your bed. Alone. Wearing this." She dangled a T-shirt —"Poke me and die." Surely she didn't mean it.

She kicked his foot and wedged the door shut. Locked it.

Then...giggled.

Oh, it was on.

Chapter 7

Mom: Is that a man's shirt in your laundry?
Cynthia: Yeah. It's from the night I took Daryl's bed and made him sleep on the couch.
Mom: I thought I taught you to share.

BLINKING OPEN HEAVY LIDS, the first thing Cynthia noted was the dark eyes above hers, staring intently. Then, the familiar smirk.

Too late, she'd already let loose a shriek.

"Nice to see you, too, honeybuns."

She wrinkled her nose. "I am not a donut."

"Honeybuns aren't either, but you're both sweet."

The cheesy line made her groan, and she closed her

eyes, only to snap them open as she exclaimed, "How did you get in here? I distinctly remember locking the door."

Disgust creased his features. "I learned to bypass those simple bedroom locks by the time I was in grade three. All you need is a butter knife."

If it was so simple, then why had he waited so long to enter?

Such a bad thought. She should be happy he'd not pushed the issue and insisted on joining her in bed. She'd have set him straight at the first amorous attempt.

Snicker. It wasn't just her wolf that mocked her.

A part of her had hoped he'd not let a locked door stand in his way the previous night. Hoped he'd slide into bed with her and...

"What are you doing?" she asked as he yanked the covers back. Clutching at the blanket to keep herself covered, she gave him the eye.

An expression he took as invitation, given he put a leg on the mattress with a muttered, "Move your sweet ass over."

Does he really think he's joining me in bed?

Forget thinking. He was, probably because she scooched over. The mattress dipped under his weight as he stretched out. Given he possessed quite a few pounds of thick, tanned flesh, encased in a lickable body, she found herself smooshed against him. She could think of worse places to be.

Or we could stay like this for a while. She could try and deny her attraction to Daryl all she wanted. Denial didn't make it true. She found him highly intriguing, sexy, and, let her not forget, arousing because, when he tried to kiss her, she melted like a piece of chocolate in the sun.

Lick me, head to toe.

Oh dear. Not exactly the right kind of thought to have when pressed against the object of her lust. He was a feline. Chances were he could smell it.

It might have proven more embarrassing if he was not sporting a huge boner, and, no, she didn't see it. She accidentally felt it.

With hot cheeks, she moved her hand away and wondered if he thought she'd groped him on purpose.

No wonder he's confused. She was sending out very mixed signals. Heck, she wasn't even sure what she felt herself.

"What time is it?" she asked. An innocuous question, something to focus on instead of how nice it felt when he placed his arm across her pillow and nudged her head onto it.

This was nice.

Must resist.

But how could she? The man was freaking cuddling! She'd never felt so blissfully relaxed and content.

And then he had to be a guy.

"I think it's time my luscious Cyn peeled the clothes from her body." Daryl ran a hand down the side of her body, tickling across her ribs. He left a trail of awareness in his wake and then had her holding her breath as he reached the hem of the shirt she'd borrowed. Fingers with callused tips brushed the tops of her bare thighs. Where would they go next?

"You want me to strip?" she muttered, her voice low

and husky.

"Totally." The full width of his hand palmed her leg, branding her. "Then I want you to stretch that gorgeous body. I want you awake and ready because..." His lips brushed her forehead. She shivered. "You need to take a shower, honey. You reek of dog and lizard. Like badly. So badly, in fact, I'm going to have to wash these sheets."

With that, he rolled off the bed so quickly she couldn't help but fall face-first onto the mattress—where she stayed, utterly mortified.

Rejected because I stink. Her wolf whined with her head tucked between paws.

Good thing one of them was feisty and wouldn't stand for it.

Oh heck no. He'll pay for that comment, she thought as she pushed herself onto her elbows. The fact that he was right didn't enter the equation. No man should ever tell a woman she needed to bathe.

And probably brush her hair, she gauged by the ginger pat of her hand on out-of-control hair. Her carefully brushed and sprayed curly do was a tad in disarray. Okay, a fuzz ball atop her head. But there were chemicals for that...which she didn't have. Rats.

"Do you have any kind of oil? Moroccan oil is best, but cooking will do as well."

He might have been talking before she interrupted, but he certainly wasn't now. Now he gaped at her with his jaw dropped. Such a cute jaw, too, with that little goatee thing he had going, the short kind that covered just the bottom, front edge of his face with a little line bisecting up to his lower lip. So sexy.

Want-to-kiss-it sexy.

"What do you need oil for?"

"Taming my curls."

For a second, he froze. He might have let out some kind of sad meow sound before he turned enough to see her. He stared. She stared right back, but her gaze did narrow when he burst out laughing. "You're talking about the hair on your head."

"Of course I am. What other curls did you think I was talking about?" At his arched brow, she got it and blushed. "That's gross. Why would I grease myself down there?"

He snickered. "Should I really answer that?"

The heat in her cheeks went up a few more degrees. "Can we stop talking about the situation down below?"

"I'd rather not. This is one of the best morning conversations I've ever had. So, do you shave?"

She pushed herself up on elbow and gaped at him. "You did not seriously just ask that?"

"Why not? Can't a man be interested in the trimming?"

"No, because it's none of your business."

"Oh, it's my business all right," he practically purred. "I'm making it my business. But on second thought, don't tell me how you garden. I am going to totally enjoy finding out myself when I pay a visit down there. With my lips."

She sucked in a breath and wanted to hold her tongue, but how could she when his words ignited her? A part of her hoped he meant it—*I want his lips to touch me* —and yet, she couldn't help but deny it. Or should she say dare him? "There will be no lips placed on my body, especially not down there."

He rolled his eyes and gave her a mocking grin. "Well duh. You need to shower and brush your teeth first."

Oh, he did not just do that. Again. "You think I stink?"

She thought he stank. Actually more like he tortured. What was the female equivalent of blue balls? Because she might have it. Parts of her certainly wouldn't stop tingling and, even at times, throbbing. He was to blame. Him and all his sexy parts.

And what did he want from her? One moment, he was seducing her with words and touches, and the next, he practically, on purpose, pushed her away.

Pushed. Her. Away.

Was he as freaked out by their mutual attraction? Did he perhaps suffer the same doubts?

Was it possible to torture him back?

Let's find out.

The plan formed in less than a second, which meant it would be a good one, one that moved so fast she didn't even know what was happening until she stood there naked.

In the blink of an eye, she'd jumped from the bed and pulled off the shirt. His shirt. The scent of him surrounded her, even marked her skin. The loss of clothing should have given her a chill, yet who could feel cold when bathed in the heat coming from Daryl's watching eyes?

Let's see just how uninterested you are, darlin'.

She looked down at her breasts. She'd not worn a bra

to bed. Sleeping unfettered was so much better, and her breasts were happy to show the love by having her nipples harden into points. Naughty suckers.

Mmm. Lips. Pulling and tugging.

Must not get distracted, even if he was. Poor Daryl. He stared without so much as blinking. His body stood poised, rigid with attention. That wasn't the only rigid thing about him.

He wants me.

It was heady knowledge. It brought out the imp in her. Since he admired her plump handfuls, she cupped them. "I see you're admiring these. Nice, aren't they? And real, too." She squeezed. He might have made a noise. "I'd let you touch, but you know"—she lowered her voice and leaned closer—"I'm such a dirty, dirty girl."

Yeah, he definitely made a pained sound that time.

She held in her smirk until she'd made it past him out of the bedroom into the main living area. From there, she noted an open doorway through which she could see tile.

Before she'd made it over the sill, she squeaked.

The slap on her ass was sharp. Crisp. Titillating and frustrating, seeing as how Daryl didn't follow through. "Don't forget to use lots of soap, Cyn. And by the way, I like the way you tend your garden. I'll be by for a picnic later."

Later? There wouldn't be a later if she killed him because, seriously, the man was begging for a maiming—or mauling, naked.

It was cat versus dog, and for every minor victory she claimed over him, he stole one right back from her.

It should have annulled her attraction for him. Ha.

Everything served to make him only more appealing. So why resist? Why say no?

Because he keeps teasing and not putting out.

Then again, so was she.

A conundrum she'd solve after she made herself smell pretty.

Then see if you can resist me, darlin'.

The shower proved refreshing, his razor sharp enough. His shampoo was some kind of inexpensive two-in-one that did little to help her hair. While the towels in the cupboard over the toilet proved clean, they held the unmistakable scent of him.

Throw it on the ground, and we'll roll in it.

Her sometimes-timid wolf didn't have a problem insisting. Cynthia settled for wrapping the terry fabric around her body, sarong style.

Wiping her arm across the misted mirror, she grimaced at her hazy face. *I look the same.*

A round face, her cheeks often called apples, and big lips that could use a dab of pink moisturizing balm. Her eyes seemed bright, perhaps more than usual. Her hair... yeah, she wouldn't talk about the hair.

She looked fine. Given what had happened, she might have expected to see some sign of her ordeal. Dark shadows under her eyes. A haunted look in her gaze. A hickey on her neck.

Okay, that was wishful thinking, and she could just hear her mother if she went home sporting one. *"Branding should be done in discreet places. But in case it happens, wear a scarf."*

Please tell me Mother has a drawer full because she

loves wearing them. Any other reason didn't bear thinking of.

Needing distraction from the fact that her parents might have, indeed, once in their lives, done something traumatizing in order to beget their only child, she dug around Daryl's vanity looking for some basics. The deodorant she found in the drawer, when sniffed, did not prove powdery fresh, but at least it gave her something to scent her skin.

Something that touched his.

She really enjoyed the application of the stuff a little too much and shoved it back in the drawer. Another drawer revealed a few toothbrushes in wrappers. She grabbed one and brushed her teeth, trying not to think of the fact that he had so many because he was a player.

Not my problem or business. He can be whatever he likes. He's not my boyfriend.

No, he was worse than that. The more time she spent with him, the more she wondered if he was her mate.

The shifter population was torn on the whole fated-mate concept. Depending on who a person spoke to, some were convinced all shifters had one perfect mate somewhere for them. Some claimed you knew the moment you met. The shock was like no other.

But then again, others scoffed at the idea of it. Mate at first sight? Never—simply animal attraction.

Cynthia often wondered if those who didn't believe had just never encountered it themselves.

Which begged the question, what did she think?

Do I essentially believe in love at first sight? At fate

drawing together two people who were meant to be together?

Or was it simply lust, and one compounded by her anxiety over her friend?

She wished for a clear answer.

Instead, she caught another glimpse of her hair.

That was at least something she could fix. She sleeked it back as best she could, and then, when she couldn't find an elastic of some sort, she ripped a face-cloth until she had a few strips, which she wove together to make a tieback. It would prevent a full-on pouf.

Since she'd entered naked, she had nothing to change into, not that she would have donned any of her dirty clothes. She had to rely on her towel to cover her.

Or strut by Daryl in the buff and see what happens now that I'm clean.

Less is sometimes better. Something her mother always said.

She ensured the towel covered all her parts—parts he'd seen, but that didn't matter. It was all about presentation. She emerged from the bathroom, the aircraft carrier roar of the fan following her, only to squeak, "There's people here!"

Indeed, Daryl had an apartment full, one of which was the big fellow they'd met the night before, who held tucked under his arm like a precious football a small dog, which she recognized as a long-haired Chihuahua with a pink bow in her hair. Pet or snack?

Beside the dog-toting guy, there was that big gator dude she also recalled. He didn't have a pet in his arms, but he did bring a smirk.

She replied with a frown as she quickly took in the rest of the strangers—a blonde-haired woman, a little boy, and another big guy with a scar on his face.

"There you are, Cyn." Daryl, leaning against the breakfast bar to his kitchen, smiled at her. "I was beginning to wonder if I needed to rescue you from drowning. I'm always ready to practice my mouth-to-mouth."

"And I love opportunities to keep my knee's aim in shape. So you might want to wear a cup."

It wasn't just Daryl that laughed. "Isn't she just Cynfully insane?"

"Enough of your screwing around. What is going on? Who are these people, and why are they here?" And why was she meeting them in a towel?

"It's a gathering of the minds, and muscle," Daryl said with a grin.

"In Daryl's case, it's the idiot," grumbled the scarred fellow. "I don't know if you remember meeting us last night. The first time, you were drooling all over the back seat."

"I do not drool."

"Really?" Daryl interjected. "A shame. But don't worry, there's lube for that." As if he'd not said something outrageously provocative, Daryl began the introductions. "You met Wes, he of the no-smile, last night. That freak over there holding this afternoon's snack..." *Yip!* "Okay, fine, we won't eat Princess today, but mostly on account of the fact that Constantine is bigger than me and likes that little furball."

"Touch my dog and I will digest you slowly." A threat

not made with much heat, and one she'd wager got tossed around often given Daryl simply laughed.

She wasn't close enough to truly scent him properly, but the apartment wasn't big enough for her to avoid it entirely. It tickled at her, reptilian in feel, but nothing like the gators she'd worked with when she interned at the zoo. "What are you?" she asked. Probably not the most polite query, but it wasn't just cats who were curious.

Constantine didn't take offense. "I'm a python."

"He wishes," snickered the last guy in the room. "I mean, have you seen the size of his dog?"

Grrr. The bite sized mutt took offense at the remark.

"Don't make me sic Princess on you," said the big snake, but it was the tiny, curled lip of the dog that proved most fascinating. Would the little thing truly attack something fifty times or more her size?

Daryl clapped his hands. "No letting Princess loose in here. Too many ankles standing on my carpet. Blood is a pain in the ass to rinse." Daryl brought his attention back to her. "That guy bugging his little brother, who isn't so little anymore, is the dead man formerly known as Caleb."

"He's also an idiot, but we like him anyway." The blonde who'd spoken waved. "Hi, my name is Renata, but my friends call me Renny. This is my son, Luke. Say hi, Luke."

The little boy never looked up from his tablet as he uttered, "Hi. Nice to meet you." Of course, it sounded more like hinicetomeetyou, but Cynthia got the gist.

"Nice to meet you, too?" She couldn't help the high note at the end. Surreal didn't cover meeting and conversing with strangers while wearing a towel and nothing else.

Shifters might have more free concepts when it came to the wearing of clothes, but they still didn't openly entertain naked. At least not the people she knew. She'd heard out west things were different, and a lot more naked.

"I brought clothes," the blonde woman called Renny said, holding up a bag. "Daryl said you needed some, what with your motel room busted up last night and the cops having cordoned it off."

So much for her suitcase and other stuff. What would she do without a wallet?

As if Daryl read her mind, he said, "I managed to sneak out your purse, but your clothes kind of got wrecked in the fight. But no worries. I'll understand if you need to wander around naked until you have a chance to go shopping."

She might have answered, but others beat her to it.

"Daryl!" Renny exclaimed.

"Yeah, Daryl," Wes mocked. "Stop thinking with your little brain and let the woman get some clothes on so we can turn our attention on the big picture here."

The big picture not including outrageous flirting with a bad kitty.

With a smile of thanks, Cynthia snatched the bag of clothes Renny offered and dove into the privacy of Daryl's room. She hurriedly dressed, and when she exited, she heard them in the midst of discussing the attack.

"By all appearances, they're back."

"Not exactly," Caleb interjected. "The dino creature can't be the same one. The lizard thing we killed a while ago is still dead. His parts are being examined at Bittech."

"What lizard thing?" Cynthia asked as she exited the bedroom.

It was Daryl who told her. "A few weeks ago, we actually ran into another one of those lizard things. It tried to kidnap my sister, Melanie, and then went after Caleb's boy." He waved to the child playing.

Caleb took over. "We had to track it down and, even then, only found the thing by luck. It was hiding out atop an almost impassable rocky spire in the swamp. At the time, we didn't know it could fly."

"Can it?" Her brow furrowed. She knew enough about shifter structure to know how exact the physique for an avian shifter had to be. Because of the huge mass involved, and strength, only those who truly kept off the weight and worked hard built the muscle needed to make it all work.

Aria could do it, but she admitted it was tough, and exhilarating. Cynthia preferred her two feet on the ground, yet her preference didn't mean that lizard thing stuck to walking.

"Flying is the only logical explanation for how this thing keeps popping up out of the blue."

"It would also explain the way the scent trails start and stop. It can simply swoop in, grab the person it wants, and fly out without triggering any alarms."

"That's all well and good," Renny said, "except lizards can't fly."

"Some dinosaurs can," said Luke, showing he was

listening more than it appeared.

"Dragons can, too." Several pairs of eyes focused on Cynthia, and she squirmed. "What? Just because we have never met a dragon doesn't mean they don't exist. I mean, look at all the stories that have them. They had to have some basis."

"Unproven fears that are given shape," Constantine said with disdain. "Dragons aren't real."

"They're making them."

This time, the eyes swung to Luke, who kept tapping at his screen, boomeranging some Angry Birds at mocking green pigs.

"Hey, little bug." Renny crouched alongside her son. "What makes you say that?"

"I heard it."

Judging by Renny's clenched jaw, Cynthia wasn't the only one chafing at the speed of the revelations.

"Heard it where, bug?" Renny asked.

Luke finally turned his gaze toward his mother. "I can't say." He turned back to his game.

Caleb knelt beside his son. "Listen here, big man, if you know something about this lizard thing, then you need to tell us."

"Why are we asking a kid?" Wes asked aloud. "Kids know nothing. He is probably thinking of some baby cartoon he watched."

Cynthia saw Caleb ready to retort, except Renny placed her hand on his arm and shook her head.

"Wasn't a cartoon." With a knot on his forehead, Luke glared. "I heard Tatum and Rory's daddy talking about how the dinosaur was a poor 'scuse for a dragon."

"Andrew? Andrew knows about these things? Why that no-good bastard." Daryl bristled as he pushed away from the counter he leaned on.

Constantine blocked his path to the door, placing a hand on Daryl's chest to prevent him from leaving. "Slow down. You can't go after Andrew based on what one little boy says. Don't forget, Andrew is the CEO over at Bittech. For all we know, what Luke overhead was part of a conversation about some of the research done on the one they've got in the labs for testing."

"Yeah, not likely," Wes volunteered. "They stopped testing."

"What do you mean? I thought they were supposed to run a gamut of blood work and tissue samples from the one we killed." Caleb frowned.

"Funny thing that. The initial results returned inconclusive. So they did them again. Lo and behold, they claim the corpse we brought them was not a lizard man but a caiman."

"That was no croc. Look at the body."

"There is no body. In order to hide it from curious human scientists working there, they had it cut into pieces and made sure none of them appeared like actual body parts. Those parts were accidentally incinerated with the other waste."

"So, there's still the pictures that were taken. Refute those."

"What pics?" Wes's smile held no trace of amusement. "They're gone. That entire folder dedicated to the creature, locked behind a secure firewall, deleted. Vanished. It doesn't even show on the backup."

"All of it's gone?" An incredulous note hued Renny's query.

"This is bull—" Caleb slid a glance over to his son. "Brown gooey stuff. The guys over at Bittech are covering it up. Someone's trying to get rid of the evidence because that was no croc. Not even a hybrid one. It kept its half-shape after death."

"Is that important?" Cynthia asked. She knew some things about shifters, but was really more knowledgeable when it came to animals.

Caleb rubbed his face, looking tired. "Half-shapes aren't something everyone can do. You have to really have a handle on the beast if you want to be able to balance equal power in the body and mind. It's not easy to do and, because it involves having a foot in each world, not meant to be. So if someone dies in the midst of it, the control slips and the body snaps back to its natural form, which is human."

"Except the dinoman stayed a dinoman."

"Did he? We now have scientists saying otherwise." Wes pushed away from the wall. "The body was destroyed, and the samples swapped for a reason. Someone is trying to prevent us from getting at the truth. The question is, who?"

Funny how a knock at the door, a firm, no-nonsense knock at such a serious moment, could result in utter silence.

Everyone looked at each other, but no one said a word as the knock came again, this time even more insistent.

Cynthia found it odd the dog didn't bark, but a

glance showed Princess was well aware there was something trying to obtain entry. Her tiny ears were pricked, her eyes intent on the door, and her muzzle drawn back over pointed teeth.

"Are you going to get that?" Constantine whispered.

Daryl jolted. "Shit. I guess I should." With a predatory grace, Daryl strode to the door and peeked through the hole. "Who is it?"

"Pete."

Who is Pete?

A question she apparently uttered aloud because Renny answered. "He's the sheriff for the town."

Daryl quickly opened the door, and a big fellow, dressed in a dark uniform loomed in the opening, filling it with his bulk. The man's jowly cheeks sported a prickly shadow that matched the short spikes atop his head. Pete gave everyone a nod and said in a low voice to Daryl, "I need to speak with you outside."

"Whatever it is you've got to tell me, might as well come in and tell us all."

"This message is just for you."

"I have no secrets."

"That's just it. You need to start keeping some," Pete snapped.

At the numerous inquiring looks, the portly sheriff sighed. "Fuck me, I need to retire. I don't need this political fucking shit complicating my life."

"What shit? What the hell is going on, Pete?" Daryl demanded.

"I don't know what the fuck is happening. All I know is I've been told to drop the investigation on that attack at the hotel, to burn my personal notes based on what Daryl told me at the scene, and I was ordered to tell Daryl to keep his mouth shut, or else."

"Or else what?" Cynthia said.

"Doesn't matter." Daryl scoffed. "I am not going to keep quiet about this. There is something seriously wrong happening here. Mutant shifters or animals or something. And they're dangerous. We need to warn the people. Tell the council and get them involved. To..." Daryl trailed off, probably because Pete kept shaking his head.

"Don't you get it yet? Who the hell do you think has the clout to call me and tell me what to do? Did you really think I'd roll over and bare my belly to just anyone?"

It was Wes who got it first. "The fucking council knows about those creatures."

"Impossible," Cynthia exclaimed. "If they knew, then they'd be wanting us to do something about it, not zip our mouths."

"And yet that's exactly where my coded orders came from," said Pete with a shrug. "I don't know who sent them, or why, but there was no mistaking the council's seal."

Most shifter groups tended to rule themselves, usually under the leadership of an alpha, or someone elected—often by battle—to keep their secret society running smoother. But while groups had a certain auton-omy, it was only because the shifter high council allowed it.

The SHC, as Cynthia had been taught, had been around for centuries, setting shifter policies in order to help prevent the spread of their secret. They acted in cases where some of their kind got out of line or brought too much attention to themselves.

Judge and executioner, without a trial. The wild nature of most shifters meant a need for speed in such matters and a swift resolution. Often that resulted in a very final outcome.

So if the council was involved in this mess and had demanded Daryl and all the others abstain, then the choice was clear. They'd have to drop the investigation.

Aria would remain lost, and those monsters would continue to roam.

Lost in her depressing thoughts, Cynthia barely noticed when Pete left. It took Daryl's clapped hands and, "Okay, now that he's gone, let's assign some tasks," for her to realize the group had not given up.

"You're going to keep looking? But what about the SHC?" she asked.

"The SHC is asking for a tribal accounting if they think we're going to sit back while some monsters prey on our town," Constantine said with a hint of a sneer.

"While those monsters roam, my family is at risk," was Caleb's reply.

"They took my brother."

"And we need to find your friend," Daryl said, finishing off the reasons.

In that moment, Bitten Point started growing on Cynthia, and a lot more pleasantly than that fungus that had claimed her razor in the motel shower.

Chapter 8

Daryl's Bumper Sticker: *"If you can read this, you better have brought the lube."*

IN DOWNTOWN BITTEN POINT later that day...

"Why did we get stuck with the library research as our task?" Cynthia grumbled. "Shouldn't that smart Constantine fellow and his little dog be here? I hate reading."

Not true. She liked reading interesting stuff. Sifting through boring newspaper articles for mentions of weird shit happening was time consuming—and didn't feature bare-chested Vikings sweeping damsels off their feet for ravishment.

Who needs a Viking when I have Daryl?

Stupid, yummy Daryl, who looked good in anything

he wore, which, at the moment, was comprised of well-worn yet snug jeans, a T-shirt that claimed he was a Bikini Inspector, and flip-flops.

The man had his own sense of style, and damned if it didn't work for him.

"Constantine would be the one best suited for this task if he wasn't working."

"What does he work as anyhow?" Atlas? The big dude who held the world up on his shoulders?

"Fireman. He's on the roster and can't just take a day off on a whim."

"I would hardly call tracking murderous lizardmen and dogs a whim," Cynthia hissed as she followed Daryl through the winding stacks of metal shelving that bore the weight of books.

"And I'm sure if he told the fire chief what we were about, he'd agree, but given we were just warned by Pete to not say a word, we thought it best we not be too blatant with our flaunting. So Constantine went to work as if everything was normal, but meanwhile, he'll be milking the boys at the station to see if anyone knows anything."

"How is that being discreet? Won't he get in trouble if he's caught?"

"Constantine knows how to keep it on the down low."

"You must be able to if you've kept the secret of shifter existence in Bitten Point so long. Is everyone in this town one of us?" Cyn asked as they passed a petite woman, her red hair caught in a loose bun. "And was that really a fox?" She craned to look over her shoulder. "My dad said they were killed off by the British in the hunts

76

overseas." She knew the smell because she'd treated a few mundane ones during her time interning at the zoo.

"A few vixens and their mates survived. They managed to make it across the ocean and settled here. They are, however, very rare. As to your other question, no, not everyone in town is a shifter. At last count, there were about a thousand residents, not counting transients and visitors. Only about half are shifters. We're too close to the Everglades and too big of a town to get completely bypassed by the humans."

"I noticed Renny's human, and she knows our secret."

"Of course she does. Not only is she mated to Caleb, but she's also a dormant descendent."

Dormant, a term often used to describe those who held the shifter gene in their body yet never managed to touch their animal. While a few youngsters manifested young, most shifters didn't fully change until their teens. Puberty was rough and hairy for those who managed to find their inner beast.

But not all could get that line of communication going. Some found their other side remained dormant. Yet, even for their inability, they were still capable of possibly passing on the gene, which screwed with those who'd chosen science as a profession and studied them because, for all intents and purposes, dormants were human.

"I can understand why Renny knows, but I've seen other humans in town, people who don't act like they know." Ignorance wasn't just a bliss. It was a smell.

"They act that way because they probably don't. I'd

say almost half the humans roaming our streets have no idea." Amazing how most folks would explain away strange things just so they didn't have to face the possibility that maybe their world wasn't what it seemed.

"Isn't it dangerous to have them around?"

"It would draw more attention to push them away. In order to maintain a façade of normalcy, Bitten Point can't reject people. We just encourage them not to stay."

"How?"

"Shitty service and food are a good start."

"But what of those you want to stay? How do you seduce them?" Innocuous words, and yet, was that a teasing smile on her lips?

"How's this for a reason?" Daryl dragged her to him and mashed his mouth against hers, catching her startled gasp, feeling the pliant softness of her lips against his.

The fire that simmered on low whenever she was around ignited. She opened her mouth and let the tip of her tongue touch his. A bold strike. A sensual one.

Flames raced through his veins and heated his skin as he sipped from her.

"Ahem." The cleared throat had them separating, but instead of showing embarrassment, Cyn's cheeks dimpled as she smiled. "I'm sorry. Are we in your way?" She threw herself on Daryl, pressing him against the book stack. "There you go, plenty of room to go around. Or did you want to stay and watch?"

It wasn't the invitation to linger that intrigued him, but the hint they weren't done.

The older woman pressed her lips tight in disapproval. "Hussy." She flounced off with a sniff of disdain.

Cyn giggled. "Wow, talk about uptight. Then again, she is a cat."

"Hey!" he protested.

With another giggle, and no repentance, she moved away from him. A shame.

"Are you going to deny felines think they're better than everyone else?" she queried.

"Why would I deny the truth?" His turn to grin.

"Such a bad kitty." She shook her head, but smiled. "This town is a mish-mash of castes."

"The bayou is just one of those places where all kinds of life flourishes, but it is also every man, cat, canine, or reptile for himself."

"I've never run into so many different flavors of shifters. Actually, I've never been in a place where the humans are outnumbered."

"Really? Where did you grow up?"

"In Atlanta."

"I thought that was big lion country?" He couldn't help his disdain for the snobby fellows enamored with their manes.

"It is, but they allowed us to live there when my mom's family objected to her marrying Daddy."

Nothing could have stopped him from asking, "Why did they object?"

"He's a bear. A loner bear, with not even one sleuth to call his own. When he met my mom, he was renting a bedroom and all his stuff fit in a duffel bag. My grandparents apparently thought he was beneath them. They forbid them from dating."

"I take it that didn't go over well."

"My parents decided to risk it all and eloped. They never went back."

"Did she regret it?" An answer Daryl really wanted to know because his own parents had followed a similar path, except, in their case, Dad was the one from the well-to-do family. His mother was considered the trash from the wrong side of the tracks. The lack of amenities and the hardness of their life eventually led to his dad leaving.

"Regret?" She laughed. "Never."

"You were lucky."

"I guess. Why do I think your story doesn't have the same happy ending?"

"Let's just say my dad missed the benefits of money and prestige. We became an embarrassing mistake of his youth."

"I'm sorry."

"Don't be. My mother said, if he wasn't smart enough to know what a good thing he had, then we were better off without him."

"So you never see him?"

"Oh, every so often he'd pop in with his fancy car and expensive gifts. He stopped, though, after we gave him crabs."

"You infected your father with a disease?"

"Not those kinds of crabs." He rolled his eyes. "We filled his expensive BMW with real ones. Turns out they're rough on leather."

How he loved the sound of her laughter.

"So you have a sister?"

"Melanie. Yeah. She's married to Andrew, who runs

Bittech Industries. They've got boys known as Terror 1 and Terror 2."

"I'm going to guess they take after you."

He adopted the most innocent expression he could. "Are you implying I'm bad?"

"Yes." She didn't even attempt to lie.

"You already know me so well, Cyn." And he wanted to know more about her, but as they'd talked, they'd reached the door to the microfiche room, to which he held the key. "It occurs to me that I never asked if your friend was a shifter."

"Aria is a bird. An eagle to be exact. But she's not bald."

He whistled. "An avian caste. We don't see many of those. I think Bitten Point currently has two that I know of. Used to be three, but one of them disappeared a few years back when we first spotted signs of trouble."

Cyn fingered the machine instead of him. Lucky hunk of metal. "And that's what we're looking for? News about old attacks? Shouldn't we be using the Internet?"

He slapped the microfiche box on the table. "Not if we want shifter news. Ol' Gary, who has to be close to a hundred, because tortoises tend to be long-lived, has been running a periodical for our kind for years now. Paper only. Limited copies. And much like some *Mission Impossible* episode, the copies are burned after being read. Except for..." He flourished his hand over the boxed film.

"And this is considered safer than having it scanned and uploaded to a Dropbox or closed online forum?" she grumbled as she pulled out the first strip and squinted at it.

"Not everyone trusts the Internet. Especially not with all those hackers who do their best to steal and dump info. The library is managed by our kind. Only a shifter can ask to see these."

"And what if a human accidentally gets their hands on them and tells the world?"

"Who's going to take this seriously?" he said, gesturing to the screen.

A picture of George Mercer, in his massive gator shape, lurking in the water, eyeballs peeking. The headline? *Bayou Hunters Target Gators and Crocs*. The gist of the article was how to play safe.

But not everything was a help piece. It talked about births, deaths—not all of them natural. Poachers were a worry for many of their kind.

Problem was, when someone disappeared, the reason wasn't always clear. Were they caught by a hunter? Did they run into trouble or find a bigger predator? Did they move on? Turn wild? Or was there something more nefarious at work?

With Cyn perched in a chair beside him, they fed the machine a page of film and scrolled through the images, each square a page from the periodical. They began with an issue starting a few years ago when the first batch of trouble cropped up.

Chili cook-off. Swamp Bite Races. Street sale. Mundane items that he quickly skipped through.

As soon as he finished one slide, Cyn had the next ready.

"This doesn't make sense," she muttered as she held a microfiche page in the air. She peered at it. "It looks like there're items missing."

"What do you mean missing? Maybe someone put the slides in out of order." He glanced over at her.

"You're misunderstanding." She pulled several microfiche sheets out and placed them in a row. Jabbing her finger at them she said, "Look." Each sheet had about twenty squares of film. The tops of them were labeled with the date the paper came out.

"The dates all line up. I don't see any missing."

"No, because the info they were trying to hide was wiped."

It was then he focused more on the individual film sheets and noted what she had. To be sure, he fed one into the machine. He quickly scrolled through the Bitten Point family picnic article. The garage sale with lots of baby stuff. Then a smear. The next page was fine. Then another smear and another. Then the rest of the paper, fine.

He swapped it for another, the week after. Same thing. Some of the film blocks were too damaged to see.

"It's like someone wiped them," Cyn said, jabbing at the screen. "You can see it used to be an image."

"Wiped on purpose, or was it an accident?"

"Well, it seems kind of suspicious. I mean, those are the dates you wanted to peek at, yet look." She pulled out some later ones, ones for the fall, after the first round of troubles died down. "See? These ones are completely intact. As are the early ones." She showed him a few of those, too. "But all of the ones over this two-month period have the wiped spots."

"It still could be an accident."

"If someone spilled something, it would smear across a few of them, not specific boxes. Someone got to these before us."

But who? The librarian seemed surprised when they told her what they'd found. According to her, no one had asked to see them recently, and they didn't keep a log.

"We need to find out what was in those missing spots," Daryl said as they left the library and emerged to mid-afternoon sunshine.

"But how can we find out? You said it yourself, the papers are destroyed."

"Unless you're a hoarder. Come on, I'm going to take you to meet Gary."

They needed answers, as more and more it looked as if a giant cover-up was in effect. Someone didn't want people digging or finding answers.

Too bad. This curious cat wasn't giving up.

Chapter 9

Cynthia: So I'm on the trail of a major cover-up and could be in danger.
Mom: This better not be an excuse to skip Sunday dinner.

THERE WERE times in a person's life when they met someone they just immediately felt connected to. Someone you trusted and couldn't get enough of.

Growing up, Cynthia had found Aria. They had that connection, but as they'd gotten older, they moved on to new opportunities—and discovered boys.

Cynthia went to vet school and found a career. Aria went through a series of odd jobs before her most recent departure on a quest to find out what she wanted in life.

Despite the fact that they led two completely

different lives, when Aria went missing, Cynthia didn't hesitate to go looking for her and, in the process, found Daryl. A man with whom she felt a strengthening connection, especially now that she was pretty sure he was one of the good guys. He and his friends certainly seemed determined to dig at what happened in Bitten Point. They were doing things, investigating, just like real PIs.

She was pretty sure that was even cooler than being a kidnapping gangster. The less exciting part was realizing there could be danger.

"Daryl?" She said his name softly and waited for him to reply. He currently thumped his hands on the steering wheel to some classic AC/DC song.

"I love it when you say my name like that, Cyn. What's up, hot stuff?"

The man had the ability to make her heart go wild with just some huskily spoken words.

"Are we in danger?"

"What makes you ask?"

"Those things that attacked my motel room the other night, they could have killed us."

"Yes, but we prevailed."

But had they? "Those two creatures were kick ass. I mean, maybe you might have done all right with them, but let's admit it." She peeked down at her curves in their snug black yoga pants and her hip-length, cowl-necked, coral pink T-shirt. "This body was made for things other than fighting."

I don't know about that. I do like wrestling. Wrestling wasn't fighting if done naked.

"You were quick on your feet."

"I threw a pillow at it." And tried to play fetch with a dogman, but she didn't mention that failure. *Because it might have worked with a real stick.* She totally believed that.

"The sheer shock of that bought you a few seconds."

"If by shock you mean mocking. But seriously, the point I'm making is those things should have been able to take me out."

"You think they were trying to incapacitate us, not kill us."

"Yes and no. I think our visitor, dogman, was trying to kill us. He came in quiet and he went after us, but that lizard thing didn't."

"It smashed through the window. It fought me."

"You dove on it. You guys didn't fight long before dogman was back."

"Then it came after you."

A totally pee-her-pants moment, but even she had to admit, "It was coming after me slowly."

"So he likes to tease his prey. Not unusual for a predator. Sometimes we like to play with our food."

"You're a cocky guy."

"More than you can imagine, Cyn."

How he made her shiver when he said her name in that tone.

"So this guy we're going to see, he's a—"

Wham!

The impact of something big hitting the car rattled her entire body. The world fragmented into a loud crash.

Screaming metal. Vivid cursing. Her head snapped to the side, and her breath whooshed from her.

Cynthia flailed her hands, not that it did a thing to help as their vehicle went screeching across pavement because something shoved them.

A glance to the side showed Daryl's jaw taut and his eyes intent. "Fuck! Hold on, honey. I'll get us out of this."

Exactly how was he planning to do anything?

Their car, shoved across the asphalt, hit the other side and then teetered along the ditch.

"Unbuckle," Daryl yelled over the noise.

"Why?"

"Unbuckle now," he shouted again.

As her fingers jumped to obey, the car tilted, enough that she could feel herself falling toward Daryl.

This wasn't good. With a click she barely heard over the crunching of metal, the seatbelt unclipped, and she lost that restraining strap. She barely had time to catch herself before the car went over almost completely. It hit the angle of the ditch on the other side, her window facing the sky.

A thump rocked the car, and it didn't take a genius to realize something had landed on the car, especially since, a moment later, a face leered at her through her unbroken window.

Crack. The window spiderwebbed as it was struck by a meaty fist.

She shrieked.

"Let me past you," Daryl demanded. He was crouched under her somehow, but with her wedged in the way, he was unable to stand or go any further.

"You want the psycho outside, you take him." To those who said she was chicken, she said try smart. Strength came from making the right decision. Foolish pride had no place here, so she let the person most capable take care of the situation.

Someone shattering the window and shoving a hand in with a gun? *More of a Daryl problem*, she thought from her spot in the back. She'd managed a quick wiggle and just in time, too, because, when that fist holding the gun dropped in through the broken window, Daryl lunged and yanked.

She preferred to not think what the cracking sound meant. Still, it didn't stop her wince at the bellow of a man in pain, a man pissed and wanting to do very vile things to Daryl.

I don't think many of his ideas are physically possible.

Undaunted by the promise of pain, Daryl laughed as the arm was withdrawn. "I'd like to see you try."

With those daring words, Daryl gripped the side of the window and, limber as a gymnast, lifted himself through.

Dude had some serious muscle.

Alone, she had to decide what to do. Only a coward would stay inside the car, and much as it appealed to hide, she had to do something.

She grabbed the front seats and poked her head through, only to squeak and yank back as a body fell atop the broken passenger side window. The head of a stranger, the hair short and almost platinum, dangled, blocking her escape...at least from the front. Here in the back, she had other options, and she rapidly took stock of them

She stood in the back, her feet on the window of the other door. She had access to a door, but she already knew if she tried to open it, gravity would work against her. Not to mention if there was another guy atop there, and he stood on it, she'd never get it open enough. But that wasn't the only way out.

I have to break this window. But how? She had no weapon, and her shoes were floppy.

But your fist is solid.

Her wolf recoiled. Ow.

Yeah, ow, but she couldn't stay in here when she could hear something happening outside.

She pulled back her fist, and her wolf snapped in her head, *Wrap it first.*

Protect it. She didn't think twice of yanking off her shirt. She wore the bra she'd salvaged from her previous outfit and yoga pants.

The fabric of her top wound around her knuckles. She pulled back and let loose, and lost her balance as her fist hit nothing.

"Eep," she squeaked, falling face first into the seat. Better than gravel. She peered at the open doorway.

Daryl stood framed in it with his feet braced on the car's body. He let out a low whistle. "Is that for me?"

A shy girl might have crossed her arms over her boobs. A saucy one would push her breasts out.

A smart woman would hold up her arms and say, "Get me out of here. I smell gas."

A stream of curse words left Daryl's lips as he

reached in to grab her wrists. He yanked her from the wreck just as they both registered the sound of screeching tires.

Standing on top of the wrecked car, she had a moment to see a black SUV scream to a stop. A body limped to it and opened the rear passenger door. The driver's window lowered, but the angle of the sun made it impossible to see inside.

Click. Flicker. A flame danced atop the lighter held in the other vehicle's window.

Surely they wouldn't dare toss it. After all, their groaning comrade was on the wreck with them.

The flame on the butane lighter didn't waver, the lit wick able to handle a little toss, a perfectly arched throw that her eyes tracked to where it landed in the bed of the pickup truck pinning them in the ditch. A pickup truck loaded with barrels of fertilizer.

Uh-oh.

Before Cynthia could scream, she was hurtling off the car, mostly because Daryl was yanking her. The landing on the ground proved jarring, but that wasn't what made her whoosh her breath. Daryl landed atop her, covering her with his body.

But the worst had yet to come.

Boom!

The world exploded.

Chapter 10

***Daryl's borrowed T-shirt from
Constantine:*** *"I heart
Chihuahuas."*

IF DARYL IGNORED the T-shirt that he'd borrowed
from Constantine to replace his shredded one, Daryl
wasn't doing all that bad.

The ringing in his ears from the explosion had
mostly stopped. The singed hair would grow back. Cyn
was spared it all because he'd shielded her, and he'd lost
his T-shirt only because they needed it to stop
the blood.

He'd not emerged unscathed from the incident.

When he'd first rolled off Cyn, the intense heat and
smoke making him hack—and, no, he did not need any

hairball remedies—he'd known some shrapnel from the exploded car and truck had hit him.

However, he was less worried about that than the inferno only yards away. The intense flames and billowing smoke saw him reaching down to drag Cyn to her feet and limp off into the farmer's field. They crushed the burgeoning stalks in their stagger until Daryl deemed them far enough to take a break.

He dropped to a crouch, facing back where they came, while Cyn sank down beside him.

"Are we safe here?" she asked.

Boom. The explosion shook the ground, but nothing rained down on them.

"I'd say yes so long as the fire doesn't start moving our way."

Given the direction of the breeze, it seemed unlikely, but with one of mother nature's deadly weapons, you never knew.

He spotted her shivering as shock set in.

"Those people were trying to kill us."

"Yes, and might not be done trying, so try and stay low. I don't know how well they can see through all that smoke, but I'd rather not let them know right yet that we made it out alive."

"You think they'll try again?" She practically squeaked the words.

He hoped not because, given their recent hardcore attempt, he might not be enough to keep Cyn safe.

A smart guy knew when he needed allies. He yanked his phone from his pocket and hit speed dial. Wes answered on the first ring.

"What is it?" Wes snapped. "I was kind of busy."

Daryl kept it to the point. "Attacked on fourteenth line just past the giant culvert. Call the fire department. And I'm gonna need a first aid kit."

"Are you all right?" Wes said in one ear while Cyn muttered, "I don't need any Band- Aids."

"A few bruises and cuts, no biggie."

"Daryl! What is sticking out of your back?" Cyn's shriek made his features pull, mostly because Wes snickered.

"See you in a few. Hope you survive."

That was in question and not because of his shrapnel hit, but because Cyn's shrieking panic might lead the killers to them.

"Why didn't you say something?"

"It's no big deal."

She gaped at him. "No big deal? There's a chunk of metal sticking out of your back."

"That might explain why it hurts a little. Pull it out, would you, and press your hands on it. It will slow down the flow of blood."

"Are you insane?"

"Impaled. They don't sound anything alike."

"I can't believe you want me to yank that thing out. You need a hospital."

"Why, when I have a vet?"

"Being a vet doesn't mean I know how to fix you in this shape." She gestured to his body.

"I'll admit there's only one long and hard shape I really want you to fix, but if that's going to happen, then first, you need to pull this piece of metal out of me. It smarts."

"Smarts?"

"Hurts like fucking hell. Now would you pull it?"

As she'd antagonized him, she'd actually been checking out the wound. He wondered if she was doing it on purpose to distract him. Did she think he was a pussy?

Nothing wrong with a majestic cat, his panther sniffed.

"Good news. The chunk isn't thick. Think sheet metal rather than spiked. And I don't think it went too deep."

He wondered if she was biting that lower lip as she gently palpated his skin. "Pull it."

"Should I count?" she asked.

"Pull it."

"Are you sure? I mean, what if—" Yank, and then another tug.

He bellowed as fabric jammed against him. "What the hell?"

"I pulled it out like you wanted."

"You could have warned me."

"I thought you didn't want me to count."

"That was before I knew you were yanking out two pieces."

"Don't be such a baby."

Was she chiding him? "I'm not crying."

"Whining is just as unattractive."

"I don't whine," he sulked.

"Sure you don't," she teased, kneeling by his side. It was then he truly noted what she wore. Or didn't.

The bra could barely contain those ripe peaches. Those pants hugged her curves.

I wanna hug those curves. And lick 'em.

An open field was maybe not the ideal seduction spot, but a man took what he had. Of course, it helped if she saw things his way.

"I don't suppose you're into kissing booboos better?" he inquired with a hopeful lilt.

"Daryl! This isn't the time or place."

"Does that mean that's a yes for somewhere else?"

"No. I mean, maybe. I mean—we're over here!" she shouted over his shoulder, having spotted the tall strides of Wes.

And there went their alone moment. It became an hour or more of sirens, along with people in official uniforms with questions. More questions. During that time, he acquired a new T-shirt and Cyn's boobs were covered—in another man's shirt. Another male's scent.

Grrr.

No amount of rubbing himself against Cyn could erase Wes's scent from it, and the jerk knew it by his smirk.

As to their story for the authorities?

Chalked down to an unfortunate accident. The pickup truck came out of the side road, not seeing them, and plowed into their vehicle. The burnt body found wedged through the window of the car was written off as a Good Samaritan thinking they were still in there and coming to their aid.

The fact that the same Good Samaritan had a gun

was glossed over. Just like the fact that Daryl was injured didn't make it onto the report.

If no one human knew about his injuries, then in a few days, when he was healed, no one would take note.

As the chaos died down, he and Cyn leaned against Wes's well-kept Bronco. A fireman in yellow pants held by suspenders and wearing a heavy jacket strode toward them, pulling his helmet off as he approached.

Constantine tossed his hat onto the fire truck before continuing their way, unsnapping his jacket as he came. "Fucking thing is hot."

"But keeps your skin baby soft," Wes snorted. "What's the word on the fire?"

"Officially, the guy driving the pickup, high on fumes from the leaking fertilizer in his truck, slammed into your car and took you into the ditch. Not realizing you were gone, he was checking inside your car when the plant shit ignited, kaboom."

"And, unofficially, we just learned that there is a connection between what happened a few years ago and now." Because there was no denying a correlation now. Too many coincidences meant something was fishy.

"I don't get what they're worried about us finding. I mean, they seemed to wipe their tracks pretty good." Cyn's two cents.

"Good or not, they were worried enough to send some guys to take us out." It still chilled Daryl to know how close Cyn had come to peril.

"If it's intentional, then doesn't that mean they knew where we were going?" Cyn pointed out. "And if they were that determined to stop us, what about that Gary we were on our way to see?

A sudden silence descended, broken by the abrupt crackle on a police scanner.

"Code 10-80. 139 Weeping Willow Lane."

"Isn't that Gary's house?" Wes asked.

Indeed it was Gary's house, on fire, with Gary in it. The old man lived, but only because he managed to crawl outside, where he passed out on the grass.

An ambulance had taken him away to the town's clinic. His age made his injuries grievous, but the stubborn coot would survive. He was too tough not to.

Gary's house, unfortunately, didn't fare so well. Amazing how an old home, with original timber frame and siding, filled with books and magazines and newspapers, burned. It burned to the ground. Not a shred of paper left. Ashes for clues and a dead end in their investigation.

With it being close to happy hour, they hit a bar where they figured there was little chance of being questioned. The only place in town where everyone minded their business. The Itty Bitty.

Of course, Cynthia didn't see the logic in their choice. She stood in shock, eyes wide as she took in the sights, before exclaiming, "You brought me to a titty bar?"

Chapter 11

Cynthia: *So I went to my very first strip joint and am thinking of trying pole dancing.*

Mom: *I hear that's how all the super models keep their figures trim.*

Cynthia: *Men threw money at me.*

Mom: *I hope you invested it into a 401. It's never too early to start.*

PERHAPS SHOUTING titty bar wasn't the best thing to do when surrounded by scantily-clad women who turned an evil eye their way.

Daryl brought his lips to her ear. "Careful, Cyn. It's just a bar like any other."

"With women who take off their clothes for a few bucks," she hissed back.

"A few bucks?" Wes snorted over his shoulder as he led the way, wending his way through the tables. "I've spent way too much of my paychecks here. Hell, I've probably singlehandedly put a bunch of the dancers through college."

"Me, too," Daryl added. At Cyn's dark look, he smirked. "Just doing my best to support my community."

Surely it wasn't jealousy making her dig her nails into her palms? "Isn't there another tavern in town? One that serves food?"

"The Itty Bitty has food, too."

"Is any of it not made in a deep fryer?" she queried.

The guys exchanged a look. "I think the peanuts aren't."

In other words, nothing healthy after the day she'd had. Perfect. "I'm in." She was starved. She felt herself shrinking...*shrinking*... She needed food. Stat!

Her revival began with a nice iced tea—touched with a little something extra—served by none other than Renny.

"You work here?" Cynthia couldn't help but blurt out.

"Tuesday through Friday until supper time. The money's decent and the tips are amazing."

"Beyond amazing," Caleb grumbled as he slid an arm around his woman and laid a kiss on her tilted lips. "Much as I might have initially disliked it, the fact is it's a decent place to work. They treat the girls here a hell of a lot better than other places."

"That's because Bobby knows happy dancers means happy clients, and happy clients keep coming back for overpriced beer."

"I come for the beer-battered onion rings," Daryl admitted as he took a seat against the wall then growled at Wes when he would have taken the other. Daryl shot Cyn a look and patted the seat beside him.

Wes and Caleb took a seat on either side while Renny leaned a hip against the end of the table.

"So what the heck happened?" Renny asked. "You guys look and smell awful."

"Car crash."

"Attempted murder."

"Trouble."

The various blurted answers all pointed to the last.

"I'm going to go out on a limb here," Wes announced, "and say that the SHC knows we're still looking into what happened."

"You think they're the ones that came after us today?" Cynthia squeaked.

"They wouldn't have resorted to hired thugs. Why would they do something so messy when they would have just sent the SHC Private Guard to pick us up?"

"Wes is right. They wouldn't have to be subtle. If they claimed we were imperiling our secret, they could have just snagged us. No, whoever came after us today was looking to make a statement."

"A pretty fucking loud one," Caleb rumbled.

"An attempt that failed, raising the question, will they try again? After all, they now know we're digging into the past. Or were. With Gary's house destroyed and the microfiche useless, have they eliminated all the sources we can search? If they have wiped all evidence, do we have to worry about them coming after us again?"

"Are we sure they eliminated everything?" As eyes zeroed in on Cynthia, she explained. "So far we've been looking for written-down accounts. Internet searches. Police reports. Reported news. You are all assuming that something was written down. But what if people were threatened back then, too? Told to keep their mouths shut?"

"Then there wouldn't be a record," Caleb said slowly. "However, the people would still know, even if they've kept silent all this time."

"If we find them and talk to them, let them know there's other people involved now, maybe they'll tell us what they saw or know."

"One big problem," Wes interjected. "How do we figure out who knows what?"

That was a problem none of them had a solution to. And they were still pondering it when the food began to arrive, served by a buxom blonde in pigtails, wearing a skirt that might have once been a bandeau in another life and a bikini top that was environmentally friendly with its lack of fabric.

Cynthia disliked her instantly, and it had nothing to do with the fact that the overly exposed woman flashed her hussy smile at Daryl and squealed. "Sweetie, it's been a few days since I saw you. I thought you'd forgotten all about me."

"Of course he did because I'm his favorite barmaid now," announced a freckled redhead with a big round tray bearing drinks and wearing tiny shorts that were smaller than most of Cynthia's underwear.

The gong show part occurred when the third and fourth woman appeared at their table to wave and giggle at Daryl while exclaiming they were his favorite.

"You're not just a bad kitty. You're a tom kitty," Cynthia exclaimed. "You're a regular here."

"Because of the employee discount," Daryl explained.

"You don't work here, do you? Don't tell me you're a stripper?" The idea shocked and titillated. She'd never gone to see any male strippers before, but if Daryl was the one taking it off...

"The only stripping I do is in private—"

"Or drunk," Caleb volunteered.

"Renny's the one letting me use her discount on the food. Their rings really are yummy. Try one." Daryl shoved the crispy tidbit at her lips, and it was automatic to open them and take a bite.

Crunch. Salty, and sweet and... "Those are freaking good." She snatched the rest of the onion ring from his hand and popped it in her mouth then took a sip of her beer.

Perhaps there was merit in coming for the food, but the flash of boobs on the stage as different girls came out every few songs proved distracting. To his credit, Daryl didn't seem to pay attention. None of the guys did.

On the contrary, Daryl showed he was most aware of her presence by the hand he laid heavily on her thigh, his occasional squeeze and gentle rub keeping her in a constant state of awareness.

Still, though, the man brought her to a strip joint. That didn't exactly scream romantic to her.

And is that what you want? Romance?

What she wanted was for those tarts to stop parading their half-naked bodies by their table and blowing kisses. It made her a touch irritable, so she let the object of her ire feel it.

"You know this whole search thing wouldn't be so complicated if you'd managed to snag one of those things the other night," she accused, noticing that her first beer seemed to have been replaced with a fresh one. She gulped another sip, the liquid courage warming her.

"What can I say? Those monsters got away."

"And you didn't go after them." She shook her head.

"Of course I didn't. I stayed with you to make sure you were alright."

"You lost our only lead." A tiny part of her felt naughty for baiting him, but just then, another perky pair went bouncing by.

Daryl didn't seem to notice. He stared at Cynthia— the winner with clothes on! "Did you escape a mental institution?

"No."

"Are you taking any drugs? Were you dropped on your head as a child?"

"No and no. Why?"

"Because only an idiot would give me shit for sticking around to take care of an unconscious woman who was just attacked."

Caleb groaned as he leaned over. "Dude. You did not just go there. Stop now."

"Stop what, poking holes in her craziness?"

She straightened after guzzling the last of her beer. "I'm not crazy. Just impulsive."

"Impulsive means you do wild, spontaneous things. Crazy means you're not firing all your mental cylinders."

"I am too impulsive."

"Really?" Daryl's eyes glinted with challenge. "Prove it. I dare you. Let's see how impulsive and sinful you really are."

"You can't just put me on the spot like that," she sputtered.

"A truly impulsive girl wouldn't have a problem."

"You want proof?" Cynthia shoved her chair back and stood. "I'm going to go on that stage and shake my booty. Is that impulsive enough?"

He leaned back in his seat and crossed his arms. "Go right ahead."

"I will." She didn't move.

He smirked. "I knew you wouldn't do it."

"It occurs to me that your dare is probably meant to distract me from the fact you screwed up and let those two thugs go free."

"I did not screw up. I was taking care of you."

"Sure you were."

The sound he let loose reminded her of the frustrated one she'd managed to get her parents to utter more than a few times.

She tried the trick that worked on her daddy. She batted her eyelashes.

"Got something in your eye?"

"Nope, but I'll give you something to eyeball," she muttered.

Welcome to logical plan number...okay, she didn't keep count, but she knew there was a good reason why she was marching for that stage—other than the beer circulating in her system—and crawling onto the platform because it didn't have any stairs she could see.

The stage was in between acts, but music still blasted, a certain recent song coming to an end leading into another one, a retro one that was rather dirty.

So dirty.

So perfect.

And not as scary as expected. Now that Cynthia stood in the spotlight, she couldn't see the crowd or the tables, just vague shadows, not that she looked for long. Cynthia always danced with her eyes closed. Gaze shuttered, arms held out to her sides, and hips rolling, she began to dance as she let the beat of "Touch Me" by Samantha Fox thrum through her body.

Her shoulders moved, rolling into her torso then down to her waist. Her ass jiggled too. This wasn't so hard.

Until someone reminded her where she was. "Take it off!"

Strip? Someone actually wanted her to strip?

Isn't that why we're up here?

Take it off. A body was a beautiful and natural thing. It wasn't something she tended to show off, but with her inhibitions lowered and her skin prickling with aware-ness—because Daryl watched—she found the hem to her shirt and pulled it over her head.

It got caught for a second on her messy bun of hair, but not for long.

With a triumphant grin, she whirled it around her head and let it loose.

Someone caught it because she heard someone exclaim, "Smells smoky."

Yeah, because I'm on fire. And not literally this time unlike the incident with the barbecue.

Her hips undulated, along with her arms, in a body wave that brought whistles from the audience.

Funny how being the object of attention could prove flattering, but not as flattering as the man who'd pushed his way to the edge of the stage.

Daryl's gaze smoldered with heat. She shook her hips and waggled her shoulders and felt a spurt of triumph— oh, yes, and heat—when a tic formed by his eye. He liked what he watched.

He wanted...

She wanted, too. Cynthia dropped to the floor and crawled to him, knowing her breasts hung heavy in her bra. The tips of them ached they'd drawn so tight. She stopped mere inches from the edge, less than a foot between her and Daryl. She could practically see the electric awareness sparking between them. She smiled and arched as she threw her head back, exposing the smooth column of her neck to him. Open invitation.

"Get down," he growled, or did she just read his lips? Did it matter? His intent was clear. He wanted her to get down? Her smile curled into something utterly wicked and mischievous as she obliged, dipping her hips to the stage and then letting a wave of sensual motion roll through her body, projecting her breasts outward. The erect nubs of her nipples poking through the fabric of her bra led the way.

The tic became more pronounced as his lips went into a straight line, but she knew it was only partly in anger. She had only to peek below his waist to see he was affected in another way.

He wants me. Much as he might blow hot and cold, that one fact remained.

But what would it take to make him finally break?

Let's find out. She pressed herself against the stage again, her hips flush with the floor, and she licked her lips as she moved in time to the music.

It was utterly decadent. Even if she still wore her yoga pants and her brassiere, she was moving in ways that left nothing to the imagination.

But some people needed visual help, hence the yelled, "Take off your top. Let's see those titties!" The request came with a shower of bills, a green paper rainfall that managed to break the intense stare between her and Daryl. It disintegrated the erotic spell they were under.

Before she could react to the request, the money, and the sudden realization of what she was doing—*in public!*—Daryl turned and grabbed the guy who'd suggested she strip further. Her very irate seeming kitty held the bulky man off the ground, and she could only watch in shock as Daryl's fist met the guy's face with a snarled, "Don't talk to my woman that way."

My woman. Did he just say that? Had he just defended her honor? Swoon because she'd never seen or heard anything hotter in her life.

Chapter 12

Daryl's other bumper sticker:
"*Get a little closer. My fist wants to talk to your face.*"

HE HAD NEVER SEEN anything hotter than Cyn on that stage, and while Daryl would have enjoyed watching more of her sensual tease, the whole punching a patron in the face didn't go over well with management, even if he was a good tipper.

With a little protest—"*Buddy was totally asking for it.*"—Daryl was escorted from the premises, but he didn't fight his ejection because, to his relief, Cynthia was right behind him.

With a pat on his back, Bruno, Itty Bitty's bouncer, told him to, "Stay out of trouble and see you in a few days."

Stay out of trouble? Where was the fun in that? And speaking of trouble, what was Cynthia thinking when she got on that stage and titillated those pervs?

You dared her, his panther reminded.

Maybe, but he never expected her to do it. Never expected the ridiculous heat that came from watching her.

Fuck, when she'd stripped off that shirt, he'd practically leaped across the room to toss a tablecloth at her. Only by the thinnest thread of control did he walk, not run, to the stage, and once there, he got caught in her mesmerizing erotic web.

A woman with smoke streaks on her face, her hair in a messy and wild bun, looking as if she'd escaped an apocalypse, shouldn't have ignited every single atom in his body. None of that mattered. He just about combusted. He almost dragged her off that stage so he could toss her over a shoulder and take off with her somewhere. Anywhere. He wanted, make that needed, to touch her.

Needed. Her. *Mine.*

"Are you okay?" Her soft query startled him from his pensive thoughts, and he whirled to face her, only to teeter as he caught sight of her shirtless, wearing only a bra. It was enough to make him want to yowl at the sky and then curse. "Bloody fucking hell. Where's your top?"

She shrugged. "I don't know. Somebody in the crowd caught it."

Way to remind him that someone else had it and was probably doing unmentionable things to the shirt. Wes's shirt, snicker.

"Put this on." He went to pull off his own shirt, but she put a hand on his arm.

"Don't be ridiculous. I'm perfectly fine with what I'm wearing. Heck, I've got a bikini top with less material than this."

She did? *Drooling is not acceptable.* Cats did not slobber like a common beast. They took action. Just one problem. There weren't many actions he could take in a freaking parking lot, in which none of the vehicles belonged to him.

"We have to get out of here, but we don't have any wheels," Daryl grumbled.

"No shit, Sherlock. It's your lucky day, though, because I've got you covered," said Wes, who stepped out of the bar and immediately lit a cigarette. A new habit? And not one often seen with shifters who, like most animals, had a healthy dislike of flames and a respect for their body. But who cared if Wes was a smoky gator? He tossed Daryl his keys. "Take my truck since your car is wrecked. I'll catch a ride with my cousin, Bruno." The same bouncer who had just escorted Daryl out.

Daryl caught the keys. "Thanks, dude. Are we going to meet up in the morning and plan our next move?" Because, despite the attack today, they couldn't give up. As a matter of fact, the deadly actions served only to demonstrate they needed to get to the bottom of what was happening in Bitten Point.

Wes took a long drag and shook his head. With smoke curling from his nostrils, he said, "I gotta go into work so you'll have to go it mostly alone. But I'll have my phone on me, so call if you and Cynthia find anything."

"Will do." Those were the last words said for a while. In silence, Daryl and Cyn got into the truck, the rumble of the motor and the static-laden western song crooning from the stereo the only sounds. He eased them out of the parking lot, driving on autopilot, the only thing he was capable of at the moment.

Today, they'd faced death, a mind-blowing deal on its own, but that wasn't what had him so fucking frazzled.

Blood simmered through his veins. Arousal heated every inch of him. The evil cause sat beside him, her hands primly folded in her lap.

As if anything about her was prim. She'd disproven that a short time ago when she practically dry humped that stage.

How wrong was it to be jealous of that worn platform?

Cyn was the first to break the silence. "Hey, if I need to stick around Bitten Point for a while, I'll have to make some cash. Think the owner of the Itty Bitty would let me do a few shifts here and there?"

"No."

"Why not? I thought I did pretty good."

She did. Much too well. "You are not working there." He growled the command.

"Why not? It's a good place to make money. Renny says the management is great with the staff."

He knew he shouldn't say it, but that didn't stop him. "You are not taking clothes off for strange men."

"Why not?"

He swerved to the side of the road, slamming the

truck into park so he could face her. "Why not? Because you are only taking them off for me."

Who said that? Since when did he care if a woman stripped for a living? Since when did he demand exclusivity?

Since I met Cyn.

Seeing her lips—those lusciously teasing lips—parting in rebuttal, he did the only sure thing to keep her quiet. He kissed her.

Kissed her with the passion that she inspired with just a tilt of her lips.

Embraced her with the fervor of a man pushed to the edge.

He claimed that mouth as his and his alone, and knew she'd succumbed when she uttered the softest mewl of pleasure and wrapped her arms around his neck.

The front seat of a truck wasn't the best place to make out. Daryl didn't care. He wasn't about to stop, not when he had Cyn right where he wanted her, in his arms.

A sinuous slide of his tongue was met by the sweeter touch of hers. He sucked at it as his hands roamed her bare skin, impeded only by the strap of her bra.

What strap? Deft fingers unhooked it, and it was simple enough to peel the offending material from her.

Her head tilted back as his lips moved in a slow glide down her taut neck. He paused over the flutter of her pulse. Rapid. Erratic. Excited. All of her was excited. The heat of her skin and the musky scent of her arousal said so.

He let his lips trail over the roundness of her breast, nipping and tasting the skin before reaching his goal.

One puckered berry. Yum.

"Daryl!" She gasped his name as he clamped his mouth over that tempting tip, inhaling it into his mouth and then sucking it, each tug making her cry out and dig her fingers deeper into him.

How her erotic response spurred him on. His erection was a throbbing ache in his pants, but he couldn't stop. *Wouldn't* stop.

He lavished attention on her other nipple, savoring the feel of it in his mouth, loving how heavy her full breasts felt cupped in his hands. He squeezed them, pushing them together so he could rapidly flick his tongue between her erect nubs.

She panted. She moaned. She even squirmed in her seat. But that wasn't enough for this curious cat. He wanted her screaming *his* name as she came on his fingers.

"Lean back against the window."

Already half turned, she complied, and for once, she didn't ask questions, just leaned against the fogged glass, her eyes shuttered, her lips ripe from kissing.

Naughty thing that she was, she cupped her breasts, even brushed a thumb over the moist peaks.

Tempting. So tempting, but he had another goal. He worked her yoga pants down, enjoying how she wiggled her hips and lifted her ass so he could pull them off enough to bare her teeny tiny panties to him. And he meant tiny.

"If I'd known you were hiding those under there..." he growled.

"What would you have done?" she asked in a voice husky with desire.

"This." He leaned down and tugged at the only thing keeping him from tasting her. The fabric stretched as he tugged, making their removal with teeth impossible. And unacceptable.

He felt no qualms about tearing the offending things from her. She was bared to him.

Much better.

Despite the cramped front seat, and the console in the way, he still leaned over to bury his face between her thighs. He nuzzled her exposed mound, humming against it, the vibration making her gasp as she clutched at his hair. Her hips wiggled, but she couldn't really spread them. Her pants, while lowered, still kept her legs tethered, giving him only a few scant inches to work with.

He'd manage. His tongue found her clitoris, already swollen. He gave it a test lick then delved farther and found the lips of her sex slick with cream.

Yum.

He lapped at her as best he could, but the space was tight, just like she was tight, he noted when he let his tongue return to her clit so his fingers could take its place.

He slid one into the heat that was all Cyn. All wet. So wonderful.

As he flicked his tongue against her pleasure button, he slipped a second finger into her, feeling the walls of her sex squeeze and pulse around them.

Tight. Oh so fucking tight.

He pumped her with his fingers as he licked and nibbled, loving how her nails dug into his scalp and she uttered soft cries. Faster he worked her, loving her erratic heart rate, heated skin, and gyrating body.

When her climax hit, she screamed his name. "Daryl!" Oh yeah! And still he kept thrusting and licking, addicted to the feel of her quivering on his fingers.

The scent of her surrounded him and drove him a little crazy. It was the only thing to explain what happened next, and no, he wasn't talking about the embarrassing fact that he almost came in his pants like some fucking virgin. He meant the other thing he did.

The bite. The mating bite. Oh hell.

Chapter 13

Cynthia: *So, Mom, a guy bit me today while we were making out. Mom? Mom? Are you listening? I said Daryl left teeth marks on me.*

Mom: *Sorry, baby girl. Just sending in the engagement notice to the local paper.*

HE BIT ME!

Now, in the normal human world, biting happened. It was a passion-induced thing or a turn-on. In the shifter world, nibbling happened, like hello, tons of carnivores here; however, there was biting, and then there was *the bite.* Some called it the claiming mark or the mating bite. Whatever a person labeled it, this one was different. For one, it broke skin, and two, a true bite bonded a pair together.

She might have wondered at that if it hadn't happened to her, the sink of his teeth into her skin triggering a second orgasm, sending her to cloud a gazillion. It was the most amazing thing she'd ever experienced, so it took her a moment to come back down and realize that Daryl was plastered against his side of the truck, looking as if he'd stuck his finger in a socket.

She would know the look. She'd done it once before, on purpose, too. Not being very old at the time, she'd wanted to see if she could become electric enough to light a bulb. She didn't, and her hair had never been the same since.

This bite was kind of having the same effect. For all intents and purposes, Cynthia hadn't changed, and yet at the same time, it felt as if everything about her had tilted.

Something in her world had shifted, and it was all his fault.

Coming down from an orgasmic high was never easy, but the headlights illuminating the cab of the truck as a vehicle pulled in behind them did help.

Daryl craned and squinted. "Shit, it's the cops. Probably checking to see why we're parked."

The why was obvious, one only had to note the steamy windows to know they were making out.

Cyn giggled. "Think we'll get a ticket for indecent exposure?" She truly was embarking on a life of crime since coming to this town.

"We won't be getting a ticket because you're going to put this on." This being his T-shirt.

She might have said no, but she had no idea where her bra was, and since she heard a door on the police car behind them slam shut, that meant they were about to have company.

Despite her short-lived stage dance, and her random query to Daryl, Cynthia wasn't too sure she was ready to embark on a life that involved showing off her naked booty—although she did enjoy Daryl's jealousy at the thought.

Quickly, she pulled the warm T-shirt over her head and tucked it over her breasts. Shiver. Even the light brush of fabric was too much against nipples, still so sensitive from his oral play. Top part covered, she also wiggled her pants back over her hips and butt, the moistness of her sex soaking the fabric. But she was covered and just in time, too, as a *tap, tap, tap*, came at the window.

Daryl rolled down the window and adopted a casual mien. "Hello, Chet. Nice evening."

"Everything all right?"

"Never better." Even she heard the false brightness in Daryl's tone.

Freckled arms leaned against the window, and a deputy's face, his green eyes dancing, peeked in. "Evening, ma'am. I take it that things are fine with you, too?"

"Yes. Not all of us are big pussies when it comes to certain things." She felt no qualms about the jab. If Daryl was going to act as if he'd committed some unbearable act, then she would totally rub his whiskered face in it.

"You might want to take your *discussion*"—small

cough—"somewhere else. It's not safe to be out and about these nights. There are things roaming."

Those words caught Daryl's attention enough to partially snap him from his glowering stupor. "What things? Have you seen something?"

Chet's fingers gripped the window, and he peered down, as if trying to decide what to say. It took him a few moments, but he raised his gaze again. "I'll deny it if anyone asks, but I know you and the lady were attacked, twice now by the sounds of it, so it's not like it's a secret. Stuff has been happening around town. Homes broken into. Women and children scared by what they claim are monsters."

"No men are reporting anything?" Cynthia interjected.

Chet shook his head. "Not that I know of."

"But that means nothing. Guys aren't as likely to run to the cops and tell them that a swamp monster scared them." Daryl shrugged and grinned. "It's a man card rule."

The deputy laughed. "My wife says it's our stupid gene."

Cynthia couldn't help but retort, "She might be right." And when Daryl protested with a "Hey," she stuck out her tongue.

"But seriously, while we've not gotten reports about anyone going missing, there's definitely something out there stalking and scaring folks."

"And taking people," Cynthia added.

"Who?" the deputy queried.

"Aria's missing."

At Chet's blank look, Daryl and Cynthia filled him in, but by the end of it, he was shaking his head. "Never even heard wind of your missing friend."

"I never technically filed a report."

"Still, though, one of our own kind comes to Bitten Point and goes missing, that should have been noticed. Where was she staying?"

At that, Cynthia blinked. "I don't know. She never actually said."

"You might want to see if you can find out if she was staying at a motel in town or if she was camping. And what about her car? Didn't you say she was driving?"

As Chet listed some things they should try and figure out, Cynthia was struck with one question that they'd forgotten to ask. "If you know all this stuff is happening, then why doesn't the town? Why isn't there a warning being issued to keep people safe?"

A grimace creased the deputy's features. "That is one of the things that's bugging a few of us. We've been nagging the sheriff to put out an announcement, even if it's a red herring one to watch for the wild dog and giant gator in the bayou. But we've been told to keep our mouths shut."

"Did the sheriff say why? Or who ordered it?"

"All he'd say was it came from above him, and that, if we didn't want trouble, we'd listen." Chet blew out a breath. "But shit, I mean, if something is coming after the folks in town, people I know... It ain't right."

No, it wasn't right, and the deputy gave them lots to think about, which might have explained Daryl's silence as they drove away. Yet the tension emanating from him was born of more than worry about the situation happening.

I think he's still disturbed by what happened, even though it was totally his fault. He seduced me. And now he clenched the wheel of the truck and stared straight ahead.

Ignore me, will he?

Not likely. He was the one who made her girl parts tingle, who made her see stars, and who'd bitten her. He'd done it, and now he thought to pretend she wasn't there? Well, two could play that game—and play it better.

When Daryl pulled the Bronco into a spot in the alley behind his place, she didn't wait for him before flouncing from the truck.

"Slow down," he snapped as she bounced up the fire escape steps, the same way they'd exited earlier.

"Make me," she sassed.

"Cyn!" He growled the words and then, a second later, cursed.

She wondered why until she breathed in. Weird dinoman smell permeated the air. She froze on the stairs and held her breath as her wolf perked its head and took a whiff.

Above us. The creature waited for them.

She didn't protest when Daryl squeezed past her. Let him face the threat first. She crept behind him, scared, but determined to have his back. Although she wasn't sure what she'd fight with. It wasn't as if her wolf would want to come out and give her a paw.

We can't let him see.

Her wolf didn't like anyone to see. Her mother and

father could claim her deformity wasn't a big deal all they wanted, but it was a big deal to Cynthia's wolf. Apparently, her furry side was afraid Daryl would turn from them if he knew.

It's not something we should be ashamed of. Yet, no matter how many times Cynthia tried to reassure, her wolf was too self-conscious.

They couldn't hide their ascent on the stairs, the metal creaking with every step. They reached the metal grate landing for his floor, only the third thank goodness. To her surprise, Daryl didn't stop at his window but kept going up, two more floors, right to the parapet of the roof itself.

More slowly, she followed, partially because that was a lot of damned stairs, but also so she could assess what was happening instead of rushing in. She stayed crouched out of sight, watching as Daryl clambered over the lip of the roof and then strode to the middle of the building. How unafraid he seemed, standing there in just pants and his flip-flops. The muscles of his back were barely visible even without his shirt, the scattered clouds hiding most of the starlight from the sky.

She might have questioned what he saw. After all, the roof appeared deserted, yet, the smell lingered.

"Show yourself. I know you're here," Daryl boldly dared it.

For a moment, nothing happened, and then, as if stepping from the shadows themselves, a figure lumbered out into the open, not close, just enough for them to recognize the towering shape, the tips of wings tucked behind, along with the oddly human and somehow alien shape of the creature.

"If it isn't dinoman. Did you come back for round two?" Daryl rolled his shoulders and cricked his neck, limbering his body.

"Sssstupid cat," the thing hissed. "You are no match for me."

"I don't know. Why not put on your human face and we'll go at it the old-fashioned way."

"I can't."

Not "I won't," but can't. Cynthia wondered at the wording as she crept higher on the ladder to better see the lizard man. While the feeble starlight wasn't much help, she still managed to note a glint of metal around the creature's neck.

"Can't show your face?" Daryl snorted. "Why not? Afraid I'll figure out who you are and come after you?"

"Who I am is not important. The town must be warned."

"Warned of what? That you're terrorizing them?"

"Not me." The thing kept forcing words out, his pronunciation chunky, as if the words were familiar but his tongue wouldn't cooperate.

"Are you going to try and convince me you're different than your buddy who kidnapped my friend's kid? You attacked me and Cyn last night. For all I know, you're the other asshole who rammed our car today."

"Not me," dinoman stated again. "She must leave. All of you must. Terrible things are..."

Before the creature could finish, his body jerked.

Even though she stood yards away, a charred smell wafted on the evening breeze.

Probably sensing his chance, Daryl darted forward, hands extending into claws, only to swipe at air. Dinoman was no longer there. The creature dove at the side of the building and threw itself into the air, arms and legs tucked tight to its frame. With a snap of unfolding canvas caught by a stiff breeze, the wings unfurled. Those massive leathery spans flapped, displacing air and keeping the reptile man's body from smashing to the ground below. With a final hissed, "Run while you can," it soared off on air currents that weren't so kind to those with two feet.

"Fuck. He got away." Poor Daryl sounded so disappointed.

Clambering onto the roof, she ran to him, uncaring if he'd been a jerk in the truck. A chill invaded her limbs, and she needed reassuring warmth.

Daryl caught her and tucked his arm around her. "You okay, Cyn?"

"Fine. But I can't help but wonder why he came here."

"To finish what he started last night." Stated as if it was the most obvious thing.

But was it? She shook her head as they walked back to the stairs. "I don't think that creature meant us any harm. I mean, think of it. He could have totally taken us by surprise. He can fly. Why not swoop at us on the stairs when he had the advantage?"

"Maybe because he wanted a bigger area to fight."

Halfway through his window, she stopped to say over

her shoulder, "I don't think he wanted to hurt us."

"He's not the good guy, Cyn."

"Are you sure of that?" she questioned, still stuck halfway in the window. "I mean, did you notice he was wearing the same collar as the dogman the other day?" It made her wonder if dinoman also wore one the previous night. Possible. She might not have noticed before on account of the whole trying-to-stay-alive thing.

"So he's someone's pet. That doesn't excuse his actions."

"No, but maybe explains them. What if he doesn't have a choice? What if someone is making him do those things? Just before he took off, I think someone activated his collar."

"I thought I smelled roasted gator. But I don't see what difference that makes. He, and whoever is controlling him, needs to be stopped."

Need. Cynthia needed a few things herself. One, to find a clue as to Aria's whereabouts.

Two, she needed a shower. In a bad way.

And three, she wanted Daryl to stop pretending something utterly wicked and wonderful hadn't just happened in the truck.

She finished climbing into his apartment and had her hands on the hem of her shirt, determined to do something about items one and two, when a cleared throat caught her attention.

Uh-oh. Someone was in there with them. Someone whose scent was so familiar she'd not initially realized they were there. She froze before she could strip her shirt and managed a weak, "Hi, Mommy. Hi, Daddy."

Chapter 14

Daryl's poster behind his couch:
Three kittens playing with yarn.
(Don't judge, it was a total chick
pleaser—and they were really cute.)

SO, exactly how was a guy supposed to comport himself when meeting a girl's parents for the first time, shirtless, still smelling of smoke—oh, and let's not forget the musky scent of pussy on his fingers and lips.

Given a certain father glared at him—and he meant glare with pointed daggers, laser beams, and maybe a few bullets—and stood well over seven feet, Daryl was less than keen to get too close.

He could probably crush my head with those hands.

Or swing us by the tail, agreed his feline.

With good reason in either case, seeing as how he'd totally gone to third base with his daughter.

Since Daryl planned to live to a ripe age—with all his body parts intact—he did what any self-respecting guy would do. He managed a gruff, "Excuse me, folks, I really gotta pee," and took off running. He also took the straightest path, and that involved vaulting over the couch so as to not get too close to Cyn's daddy, and dove into the bathroom.

Safety. Ha ha! He'd made it. He shut the door to the facilities and leaned against it.

A rabid bear didn't come charging through. Things were, while not yet looking up, at least not getting worse.

Could things get any worse?

He'd bitten Cyn. Had the most erotic moment in his life. Ran into her father. Seen one possible future, and it was crushing. Literally.

Exactly what direction should he take to stay out of trouble?

Did a safe path even exist?

Since when did he care about safety? This feline lived on the edge. Danger and adventure were practically his middle name. No, seriously, he craved adventure, given his job as a construction worker wasn't all that exciting, but it was great for keeping him tanned.

Can't tan if I'm six feet under. And before anyone went calling him a pussy, the guy towered at least seven freaking feet! Add in he was Cyn's dad, and Daryl was screwed without lube.

"Shit." Realizing he'd said it out loud, he leaned over

and turned on the tap. With the rushing sound of water covering his actions, he muttered a few more choice curse words.

What were her parents doing here? How the hell had they gotten into his place? Should he hide in here until they left? That seemed pretty chicken, even if he was fifty percent sure Cyn's father would try and kill him.

You also forgot the part where you abandoned Cyn.

It's her parents.

Even worse.

Fine. He'd have to go back out and save Cyn, but he couldn't go out smelling like he did. Having experience with mornings where he hit the snooze button one too many times, he was well experienced when it came to quick bathing. He stripped and jumped into a shower that started out cool since he didn't wait for it to heat. The bar of soap lathered his skin, leaving it fresh smelling —a shame, he rather enjoyed wearing Cyn's scent on his skin. Maybe he'd rub against her later.

Lick her again.

Great idea.

She is our mate.

Bang. He wondered if anyone heard him rap his forehead off the tile wall. It was hard to war with a lifetime of casual affairs to a ridiculous certainty she belonged to him.

Mine.

Help.

He pretended he didn't whimper that word as he rinsed. The towel hanging on a hook provided a handy dry, but he couldn't go out wearing it. Given his washer and dryer were in the bathroom, hidden behind folding doors, he managed to find some clean clothes. Wrinkled, but who cared? At least he smelled more presentable, not that Cynthia seemed pleased that he'd washed away the evidence of their dalliance.

As he stepped from the bathroom, wisps of steam misting about him, she tossed him a tight-lipped look. *The look.* A look that men all over the world feared.

His mother used that look on him as a child. It still worked, but wow, was it even more frightening on Cyn's face.

"Feeling better?" she snapped as she crossed her arms over her chest. She also cocked her head, sending her untamed hair flying. So much hair. He loved it. Wanted to grab it and pull it and...

Um. Yeah. Not exactly the right time to be thinking about that. Big head, stand down. Little head, use some of that brain matter before he was doubly murdered, probably by Cyn first.

He made an attempt to alleviate the tension. "I feel much better, thank you."

"Awesome, because Daddy has some questions for you."

"He does?" Because it looked more like her daddy had an ass whooping waiting for him.

"I'm sure you won't mind telling him how we hooked up and what we've been doing." He caught the barb she sent his way and could have kissed the smirk teasing her lips. "My turn to strip out of these clothes and get clean," Cyn announced as she skirted her parents for the bathroom. As she brushed past Daryl, she murmured, "Hope you have a few lives left, darlin'."

With those reassuring words, she closed the door and left him alone with *the parents*. Dum-dum-dum. Did anyone else hear ominous music playing?

"You must be Daryl," said the woman. Where her husband was big with a dark complexion, she was short and rotund with pale skin. She also had the wildest honey brown hair, totally at odds with her prim knee-length skirt and perfectly pressed blouse.

"I see where Cyn gets her smile and gorgeous hair from."

A hand reached to pat it. "Thank you. It runs in my family. I prefer to keep it tamed, but Larry likes it like this."

"He doesn't care about your hair, Eleanor. He's trying to kiss ass because he's gotten our baby girl embroiled in something dangerous."

"I have not. It just kind of keeps happening," he added with a shrug.

"How did you meet?" Eleanor asked, her eyes bright with rapier interest.

Should he mention the whole kidnapping thing? Exactly how much did Cyn's parents know about her current quest to find her friend?

"We met over drinks." *And then went back to her motel room and slept together.* He didn't mention that part mostly because that platonic evening with a hot woman would totally ruin his reputation as a bit of a ladies' man. *Rowr.*

"Drinks, eh?" The stare narrowed.

Translation: *You thought you could get my daughter drunk and put the moves on my precious baby girl.*

Was it too late to run for the window and the swamp?

His cat smacked him with a furry mental paw. He could handle this. "Cyn came to the bar looking for people who might have seen her friend. She recognized me from a photo. We talked about it. Once Cyn realized I had nothing to do with Aria's disappearance, she agreed to let me help her."

"And do you help all young naïve girls by having them come stay with you?" A dark brow arched, and teeth were bared.

Even if Cyn's father stood with a leg in a walking cast, Daryl didn't doubt the man could hurt him, hurt him badly, especially since Daryl couldn't, out of respect to Cyn, hurt him back.

Fuck.

"Larry, stop teasing the poor boy. I'm sure he's got nothing but honorable intentions toward our girl. Right?" Eleanor's bright eyes pierced him.

"Um." He knew what the right answer was. It was on the tip of his tongue. It showed on the marking on Cyn's inner thigh. He just couldn't say it aloud. Saying the words "Cyn is my mate" would irrevocably change things.

Yet didn't things change the moment I touched her?

Before Daryl could blurt something that would probably see Larry's granite fist meet his face, a phone rang. More like sang "Hotel California" by The Eagles.

Three sets of eyes went to the smartphone dancing on the counter, a cord dangling from its charging port. It was Cyn's phone, left behind on their excursion today so it could charge its totally dead battery.

Should they answer it? The song seemed to taunt them to do something. But still, none of them moved.

Steam preceded a certain irate mocha hottie as she stalked from the bathroom, wrapped in a towel. "Are none of you capable of answering?"

No, they weren't, since a smiling face and the name Aria lit up the screen.

For a moment, Cyn's face blanched, and then she recovered and snatched at her phone answering with a, "What the hell, Aria? Why haven't you been answering? You scared the poop out of me."

There was an avid listening audience as Cyn turned to lean against the counter, phone held out, the speakerphone activated. She didn't need to put her fingers to her lips for them to know to keep quiet.

"Sorry, Thea. I've been roughing it the last few days. Communing with nature and all. You know how I love to sleep under the stars."

Everything sounded fine so far to Daryl, yet for some reason, Cyn's lips pursed. "Yeah, well, you had me worried. You usually call every day."

"Shit happened. I was just calling to let you know I am fine."

"Where are you now?" Cynthia still bore that crease on her forehead. The tension practically oozed from her.

"Here and there," was Aria's vague reply.

"Are you in Bitten Point?"

Even Daryl, who'd never met Aria, knew that the

laugh she uttered was fake. "I'm long gone from that place. Just wandering the road."

"Listen, why don't we hook up? I took some time off from my practice. You know, the stress and all. Why don't I join you? We can have a real Thelma and Louise adventure."

"You can't do that." The most starkly said thing so far. "You should stay home. I'm busy. Real busy."

"Busy doing what? Aria, is everything okay?"

The rustle of a hand covering the receiver was very noticeable, as was the sudden silence as the call was muted on Aria's end.

It didn't take a genius to decipher the agitation in Cyn as she twirled a wet strand of hair on a finger, as if her curls needed any help.

When Aria returned, it was abrupt. "I'm fine. Everything is fine. I've met a guy. A hot guy. He's traveling with me. That's why you can't come. Maybe next time. Listen, I gotta go, Thea. I'll try and call you in a few days, but if I don't, don't worry. I'm having the time of my life."

"Then tell me where you are," Cyn whispered. "Aria—"

Her friend cut her off with a rushed, "Bye." Then the line went dead, and Cyn's knees buckled.

She didn't hit the floor. It took Daryl leaping and diving so he hit the floor first, but better he take the impact than Cyn. Injury averted, he squirmed to a seated position, holding her on his lap.

"Come on, Cyn. No need to freak. At least we know she's alive."

Obviously Aria had managed some kind of covert

message because that was the only explanation for Cyn's distress. "You don't understand. That conversation, all of it was fake."

Her father dropped to a knee, the one in the cast outstretched, and touched Cyn's cheek with a ham-sized fist that was rough in texture yet gentle in its touch. "Baby girl. Don't you worry about Aria. Daddy's here, and we'll make sure she's safe."

Eleanor sniffed. "Of course we will. The nerve of keeping her prisoner. Don't they know she's the second daughter of my heart?"

Cyn sniffled. "How will we find her?"

"First thing in the morning, we'll go looking for where she stayed and her car."

"She rides a motorcycle," Cyn said.

"Whatever. Chet's right. We should have been looking for where she was staying. Maybe then we'll find a clue."

"Sounds like a fine idea," Eleanor exclaimed with a clap of her hand. "We'll see you in the morning."

Larry turned his head to address his wife. "What do you mean we'll see them? Thea's coming with us."

"To stay where? Our hotel room only has one bed, silly bear."

"So we rent another room."

"The hotel is full," said Eleanor through gritted teeth. She grabbed her husband's arm. "We should go. Let these two rest. Here. Alone."

Why did Daryl shiver when Eleanor winked at him?

Larry got to his feet and glowered down at his wife.

"Go? We did not drive six hours for us to just leave our daughter with this—this—"

"We are leaving *now*." Spoken with utmost steel at odds with the sweet smile Eleanor turned Daryl's way. "We'll see you two tomorrow morning." Gripping her husband by the arm, they went out the door, leaving them alone but still able to hear Larry's muttered, "I don't like it."

"I know, dear. Get over it. And hand me your phone. I need to post a status update."

Still seated on his lap, Cyn groaned.

Daryl immediately turned his attention to her. "Honey, are you all right?" Had she hurt herself falling against his rock hard body? Fact, not much conceit.

"I'm fine, but not for long, and neither are you. You do realize that my mother is now announcing to the world that we're sleeping together?"

"But we aren't." Yet, which was splitting hairs.

Cyn let out a very unladylike snort. "My mother doesn't care about those kinds of details. She just found me with a guy, in his place, wearing his shirt, looking like we just fooled around in a firepit. You're lucky she didn't start measuring you for a tux."

"So we'll set her straight."

"Good luck with that."

Did Cyn have to giggle when she said it?

To change the subject, which was veering uncomfortably close to the thing he'd done that should not be named, he said, "We should talk about Aria's call. Even I could tell the entire thing was bullshit."

Widening her eyes, Cyn glanced at him. "You didn't buy it either?"

"Not for a second."

"Good because the whole thing was bogus. Aria hates camping, and I mean hates it with a passion. She is a girl who loves a soft mattress with cleans sheets. Also, if she were going to hook up with a guy, she would have told me. In today's world, a girl can't be too safe. There's a lot of freaks and psychos out there, so the first rule of dating is to let someone else know who we're seeing."

"Did you tell anyone about me?" He could have slapped himself for asking because he'd just implied they were involved, which they were. But still. Fuck.

"Of course I did. I told my mom. Who then announced it to the world on Facebook."

Good thing he didn't believe in social media, although it might explain the congratulations he'd gotten on his way into the library with Cyn today.

"Speaking of your folks, why did they show up? Because you sure as hell never mentioned they were coming."

"You'd know why if you'd stuck around instead of running with your tail tucked to have a shower and abandoning me to papa bear and mama wolf," she accused, firing him an intense glare.

"They're your parents," was his cop-out.

"What man leaves a girl he just dragged to a strip joint to get interrogated by my dad?"

"A smart and still living one." There wasn't an ounce of repentance in his reply or grin.

"You are a bad cat."

"The baddest, honey. Feel free to punish me anytime." For a guy determined to try and slow shit down, he kept daring her to touch him.

Yes, touch me.

Instead, she snorted. "You wish. Now that my parents are gone, you're all Mr. Suave and Sexy, but I haven't forgotten your cold shoulder in the truck. What the heck was that about? Did my *garden* not appeal?" She wasn't about to let him off the hook, it seemed.

But how to explain that the fact he'd lost control enough to mark her scared the living fuck out of him? Like seriously scared.

Was he ready for the type of commitment a mating entailed? One woman, one pussy, one person to go home to for the rest of his life?

Until we have cubs. The reminder did not reassure, but rather than shy away from her and use the opening she gave, he reassured her. "I've never played in a nicer garden." *Argh. Shoot me now.*

"Shooting you would be too kind."

Oops. She wasn't supposed to hear that. "I'm feeling really uncertain right about now."

"And I'm feeling rather uncomfortable in this wet towel."

Was she really? Because he was rather enjoying the fact that they were both still sitting on the floor, him a lap for her to cuddle in.

Wouldn't I enjoy it more, though, if she took off the towel?

Fucking right he would.

Slam on the brakes.

Why couldn't he stay in control for five minutes where Cyn was concerned? *Let me have some semblance of pride or a choice.*

Except it seemed there was no choice. Much as it might terrify, there was something happening between the two of them. Something he couldn't seem to stop, and really, did he even want to?

With Cyn, he came *alive*. What kind of idiot would throw that way?

Chapter 15

Cynthia: *So I slept with Daryl.*

Mom: *Might I remind you that a true lady saves herself for the big day, or at least until she gets a ring?*

Cynthia: *Um, Mom, I saw all the scarves you wore in those pictures when you were dating Dad.*

Mom: *So I hear the local restaurant serves a lovely crab cake.*

I'M SUCH AN IDIOT. Or a masochist. No matter how many times Daryl blew hot and cold at her, Cynthia couldn't help but want him.

At times, she wondered if he suffered the same confusion over what happened between them. Did he also struggle against the undeniable pull drawing them together? She would have thought the bite mark made things clearer, but instead, it had made things worse.

Do I want him?

Yes.

Then why did she still fight it? Why fight what they both wanted?

Why indeed? It wasn't as if they had anything else to do. The hour was now too late to allow for a proper search, and she could admit, to at least herself, that she didn't feel safe outside in the dark. Then again, today proved the daytime was no safer.

She had almost died today in that car crash. Then almost died again when Daryl's dexterity with his hands and tongue brought her an ecstasy that stopped her heart for an eternity or two. She certainly remembered being unable to breathe.

She definitely wanted to do it again. She wondered if the intensity and pleasure were a one-time deal? Could they even come close to replicating what they'd shared a second time?

She wouldn't mind finding out, and since they were in for the night, no time like the present to find out. The questions now was, take the bold or sly approach?

She couldn't have said if it was chance or intention that her towel got snagged when she stood from his lap. Did it matter? She added an extra swing to her hip as she walked away from him to the bedroom.

He might have made a strangled sound. He definitely didn't sound all there when he remarked, "Cyn, you seem to have lost your towel."

She tossed him what she hoped was a coy look over her shoulder. She couldn't be entirely sure of the effect, given she felt her hair drying in a fluffy mane around her head.

Hard to worry about hair, though, when she stood completely naked in front of a guy who'd just jumped to his feet and stalked her, and she meant stalked. Every step measured, his eyes practically glowing and smoldering with erotic intent.

He stopped barely an inch from her body. Head cocked, she met his stare, licked her lips, and threw herself at him when his arms wrapped around her, yanking her off her feet for a kiss.

How he confused her with his mixed signals, but dammit, that didn't mean she resisted his touch.

Their passion was wild, almost violent in its intensity. He might have rammed her against the nearest wall, or she might have dragged him there. Either way, her spine pressed into the firm surface, her legs spread at the insistent push of his thigh. His hands held her pinned, feet not quite touching the ground.

She devoured his lips, loving the taste of him, loving the sizzling passion that never failed to erupt every time they touched. A passion that seemed to grow, not lessen with every new caress.

"You're driving me completely mad, Cyn," he rumbled against her lips.

She nipped him and murmured back, "It's not that bad once you get used to the strange looks."

"I want you so fucking bad it hurts."

"Then why aren't you doing something about it?" She let her lips travel the length of his rough jaw then down the strong column of his neck. She sucked, unable to prevent herself from leaving some kind of mark on his skin.

Marking him as mine.

He didn't seem to mind because, head tilted back, he groaned, even as his leg moved slowly against her, the fabric of his pants a welcome friction against her moist sex.

She let out a small cry of surprise as he lifted her higher, enough that her legs could wrap around his waist. He slipped a hand between their bodies, finding her trembling core and sliding a finger in.

She clenched at him, wanting more. Wanting him. His cock. Inside her. Thrusting. Now!

A sound of frustration left her lips as her questing hands couldn't quite reach far enough to rid him of those annoying pants.

"Need help?"

"I need you." She said the words without even thinking, and he sucked in a sharp breath.

He also acted. The finger left her channel, the whir of a zipper filled the silence, and the hot head of his shaft slapped against her a moment later.

As he rubbed the swollen tip against her nether lips, she couldn't help but shudder. Anticipation made her muscles tighten so that, when he went to slide the head of his dick into her, he had to push, her snug sheath too excited to relax.

While one hand gripped her ass, the other cupped

her face, drawing her to him for a kiss. How that man could kiss. Exploring and nibbling and teasing.

She sighed, and he slammed his cock home.

Sweet heavens, yes!

She locked her legs tight around him and snared him as well with her arms, keeping him close, loving the decadence of his T-shirt against the bare skin of her upper body. As he thrust, quicker and quicker, his kisses slowed until, with a groan, he rolled his head back. The cords in his neck bulged. He was holding off, holding off for her.

Not for much longer. She was right there, on the cusp. Each time he buried himself to the hilt, her pleasure edged higher.

She licked the exposed part of his neck, humming against his skin as he pumped her hard and fast. In and out, he slammed his cock, not too rough, but not too gentle either. Hard, fast, and passionate, just the way she wanted him.

"Give it to me." Did she growl it aloud? He certainly took things to the next level, and her sex gripped him, fisted him tight.

And then he changed the angle, just a little bit. He hit that sweet spot within her.

That did it. "Oh my God, I'm coming."

She burst. At least that was how it felt, as if a dam in her had opened, letting pleasure swamp her with wave upon wave. It was too much. Too much. Too...

She bit him, her teeth latching to flesh and holding on as she kept shuddering and groaning. She didn't let go, even though he yelled her name, "Cyn!" and came with hot spurts.

Together they clung to each other, wrung weak by the tsunami of bliss. Shaking with the aftermath. Then sinking to the bed he carried her to, still entwined. As she placed her head against his chest, she smiled as she thought of her next call to her mom.

Cynthia: Yeah, so what should I do if Daryl needs a scarf to hide something?

Mom: Why would you hide it? Let the ladies and tramps know he's off the market.

Chapter 16

A T-shirt a friend ordered for
Daryl after meeting Cyn:
"Screwed with a great big silver
Philips head."

WAKING the next morning with a luscious mocha honey against his body? Awesome.

Seeing his neck in the mirror after he took care of business in the bathroom?

"What the fuck? Cyn! Cyn!"

He bellowed her name as he stalked to the bedroom then almost fell over his suddenly ungainly feet because she rolled in his bed, flopping onto her back. The sheet pulled away during her twist, and she'd not dressed after their playtime—_Rowr_! What this meant was a stunning display of breasts. Breasts he knew intimately.

We should go over and say hello again.

No, he had to focus. He needed to have a serious talk with Cyn.

It's too early to talk.

Yeah, and according to his panic, too early to get serious about a girl.

Say that to the bite you left on her thigh.

Excuse him, but they were talking about her lapse in judgment, not his. "Do you know what you did?" The words emerged a tad growly.

"I know, and I enjoyed." She licked her lips and winked. "But I gotta say I thought only roosters crowed at the crack of dawn." Pulling her arms overhead, Cyn stretched as she yawned.

He couldn't help but stare, harden, and desire. Maybe he should get back in bed with her?

Stay strong.

The sheet slipped farther, showing the rounded swell of her belly, the indent of her waist, the top of her garden.

Meowr? Such a pained sound, and it came from him as she flashed him. But he would resist. He'd seen boobies before, and just because hers were splendid was no reason to forget his complaint.

"Don't you try and distract me," he said, wagging a finger. He pointed at his neck. "Look at what you did."

"I see it." She smiled.

Did she not understand the gravity? Perhaps if he explained. "You bit me. Why would you do that?"

"Why wouldn't I?"

"Because you shouldn't have." Weakest reply ever and it wiped the smile from her face.

"Well, that's priceless coming from you, seeing as how you bit me first." She crossed her arms over her chest, but under her breasts, causing them to plump. It also pushed them together, creating a mysterious valley —*that is really begging to get explored, with my tongue.*

Argh. She was doing it again, playing dirty, and the blood fueling his brain fled south, which was why he made the colossal error of saying, "That bite was a mistake."

The narrowing of her eyes almost saw him take a step in retreat. "A mistake?" She flung back the sheet, spread her thighs—*thighs that were wrapped around my waist last night*—and pointed to the perfect crescent on the inside of her thigh. "Do you often make mistakes like that?"

"No." Because he wasn't even entirely sure it was a mistake. A part of him screamed this was right. She was right. And perfect. Yet... "I'm not ready for this." He could feel the panic clawing at him. Or was that desire because, really, instead of an urge to run from the woman who challenged him, he wanted to dive on her?

Oops. Wait, he did. He yanked her arms over her head and pinned her to the mattress.

"Now what are you doing?" she asked, trying to sound cross, but instead coming across as slightly breathless.

"Saying good morning hopefully without my foot first."

"I really wish you'd make up your mind on what you want."

"You." Yeah, the word slipped out.

Her eyes widened, however she didn't have a chance to reply as his phone chose that moment to ring. He dove on it before he had to deal with his admission. He should have checked the number first.

"Hi, Mama." Practically said on a sigh.

"Don't you hi me, *gatito*."

It was too much to hope Cyn didn't hear. The giggle said it all.

No matter how many times he begged—and pleaded with his biggest eyes—his mother kept calling him *gatito*. Translated: kitten in Spanish. He was a grown man. It just wasn't right.

His mother didn't care if he thought it emasculating, just like she cared too much about his love life. "What is this I hear about you seeing a woman?"

"You know I don't believe in dating."

The hot glare between his shoulder blades practically turned him into ash.

His mother sniffed. "It is only because you have yet to find the right woman, *gatito*. Your sister says you are living with a girl you just met."

"No, I'm not."

A cleared throat as Cyn objected. Damn her acute hearing.

And damn his mother's sharp ears, too. "Are you going to deny a woman has been sleeping at your place the last two nights?"

"Okay, there is a girl staying here. But it's not what you think."

"Two nights. And you've been spending the day with her. Don't deny it. My sources saw you."

"I really wish you wouldn't spy on me."

"What else is a mother to do if she wants to know what her son is up to? A good thing, too, or I wouldn't know you'd gotten serious with this girl."

"Who says it's serious?"

His mother let out a very unladylike snort. "You let her sleep over. Twice."

"You make it sound like I only have one-night-stands," he hissed into the receiver, feeling heat roasting the tips of his ears.

"Those girls you're dating might as well have been. You never brought them to your place."

Because he had this thing about sleeping alone, a rule he'd now broken and didn't regret.

He flashed a glance at Cyn and caught her smiling smugly.

"You're reading too much into this. I'm just helping her out with something."

Cyn snickered before she drawled, "You've been helping me all right." And, yes, the minx did wiggle on the bed and wink.

"Can she cook?"

In the bedroom, totally. But that wasn't what his mother wanted to know. "Listen, Mom. I gotta go. I'll talk to you later."

"Love you, my *gatito*."

"Love you, too, Mama."

A man wore his embarrassment as a badge of honor. He spun to face Cyn, who grinned. "Who's a cute gatito? I would have never pegged you for a mama's boy."

"I am not." Much.

"I won't judge you for it. I'm sure there's no way your mother is as bad as mine."

I wouldn't wager on that.

The phone rang again, a soundtrack from the *Minions* movie. He didn't even have to look at the number when he answered. "Hey, Melanie."

"Who's Melanie?" Cyn mouthed, an irritated look on her face.

"It's my sister," he mouthed back.

The beaming smile proved very distracting, which was why he turned away again, but it didn't stop his sister's whispered, "Is that girl you've been hanging out with there right now?"

Amongst shifters, who possessed rather decent hearing, secrets were hard to keep and conversations were rarely private.

Before Daryl could reply, Cyn did, loudly and with a mischievous glint in her eye.

"Hi, I'm Cynthia. Your brother's been helping me look for my friend Aria."

Daryl held the phone away from his ear as his sister shouted, "You're the girl Renny and Caleb have been helping."

"Along with Constantine and Wes," Cyn added.

"Wes is working with you, too? Not that I care," his sister quickly added.

At this point, he realized who was the third wheel.

Daryl held out his phone and, in his most sarcastic tone, said, "I'm sorry. Am I getting in the way of your talking to my sister?"

It wasn't just Cyn who said yes.

He could only gape as his honey grabbed the phone, tucked it to her ear, and began chatting with Melanie.

Blink.

This wasn't happening.

First his mother meddling in his love life, which should be noted wasn't new, but usually his mother tried to fix him up with the daughters of friends, girls Daryl never bothered with. This was the first time his mother had taken an interest in a woman Daryl found on his own.

Actually, she found me. And he'd not been able to stay away from her since.

Shit. How did that happen? How could he not be tired of her yet? Or ready to have some alone time and "me" space?

To the sound of Cyn and his sister talking, he wandered out of his bedroom, utterly bemused. Only a day or so ago, he was a single swinging bachelor. He'd almost earned his own table at the Itty Bitty he enjoyed the entertainment so much.

He had a feeling Cyn might have ruined him when it came to breasts and half-naked women.

Despite how hard he tried, he couldn't remember a single exotic dancer now that Cyn had taken the stage, not only in his memories, but his heart, too.

All he saw when he closed his eyes was her. The

recollection of her splayed across his bed, skin a tempting chocolate, lips so berry bright and plump.

We should break the phone and give her a proper good morning. Maybe nibble on that other thigh.

Argh. No. Slow down. Going to her now would admit something, something he was still in denial about. A man needed coffee before dealing with relationship woes.

As he sipped the hot brew—with eight cubes of sugar, cream, and then a cement mixer to stir the sweet sludge— he listened to Cyn chatting and laughing with his sister.

A few minutes later, she wasn't laughing as she strode out of the bedroom, phone in hand, utterly naked. "You never told me you had twin nephews."

"I told you I had nephews."

"Yeah, but you neglected to mention they were twins. Do they run in the family?"

Couldn't they talk about something else, such as her need to put on a nun's outfit? But no, she continued to taunt with her nakedness, and the glint in her eyes said she wanted an answer.

"Twins tend to run on my dad's side."

Cyn frowned. "You could have warned me."

"Warned you? Why would it matter?"

She arched a brow and cocked a hip, which proved rather interesting, given she did it naked. However, his distraction didn't mean he missed her words, but he still made her repeat them.

"I said you didn't use a condom. So unless *you're* on the pill, then babies are a possibility."

A man was entitled a long blink while he processed

this. He could even hyperventilate a bit. Babies? No. Oh hell no. Yet, she was correct. They'd skipped protection. Daryl rarely used condoms because his kind proved impervious to most diseases. As for pregnancy... "Aren't you on the pill?" Wasn't every woman nowadays taking it? The hormones in it worked on shifter females. They just needed a much stronger dose.

She shook her head, sending her hair fluttering. "No, I am not. I don't like the way it makes me hairy."

"But... We... That is..." He couldn't say it aloud, let alone contemplate it.

"Had sex. I know. And now I could be pregnant because someone didn't pull out."

He stabbed at his chest. "You're blaming me? You could have told me you weren't taking anything."

"I might have except I was kind of lost in the moment, which, again, is totally your fault. And, besides, what guy doesn't use one until he knows for sure?"

A guy who was also lost in the moment. "It was just one time."

"One time? One time could mean twins in there." Her turn to poke herself in the belly. "I know we've marked each other, but that's a bit quick, kitten."

"Don't call me kitten."

"Why? Does it make you think of your mommy?"

No. Cyn definitely didn't invoke any maternal thoughts, but she sure did ignite carnal ones.

A woman indicating she might be with his child should have sent him fleeing. Running for the swamps to hide.

Not this kitty.

This kitty found himself stalking toward her, drawn despite himself.

As for Cyn? She didn't flee. On the contrary, she also moved, and neither stopped until they were pressed against each other. Since he wore only boxers, nothing could stop the sizzle that arced between their bodies. Their gazes caught.

"I think we can both agree there is something happening between us," she stated.

He nodded in agreement.

"I'm not sure where it's going, but for the moment, I'm going to stop fighting it. Are you?"

"Is that wise?"

She smiled. "Are you seriously asking the crazy girl? No, it might not be wise, but I'll be honest and say I've never experienced anything like being with you."

"Me either."

"So why don't we agree for the moment to just enjoy ourselves, find Aria, and then see how things pan out? Maybe go out a few times, hang out."

"Are you talking about dating?"

"Which sounds kind of backwards, given we've munched on each other's skin and shared a bedroom, but yeah, we should *date*." She winked as she sashayed to the bathroom, her round buttocks tempting.

He couldn't help but stare, and kept staring long after she'd left his side. He visibly startled when she stuck her head out the door and sighed.

"In case you're that oblivious, that was an invitation to get your ass in here. We could both use a shower. I promise I'm very dirty."

He wasn't oblivious, just overwhelmed, but not so much that he didn't get his ass in that bathroom. It was a good thing they had lots of hot water because she got plenty dirty before she got clean.

Just in time, too, as insanity came to plague them again.

Chapter 17

Cynthia: *So thanks for letting Daryl and I have some time alone last night. We managed to get a few things talked out.*

Mom: *So he proposed?*

Cynthia: *No!*

Mom: *Why not?*

IF ONLY CYNTHIA WERE EXAGGERATING. Poor Daryl, she'd given him hell for not warning her about the twins in his family, but then again, she'd not truly fully cautioned him about her parents.

Tit for tat, and something they'd have to deal with if they did stay together. She'd have to live with his genetic disposition that might see any fertilized eggs of hers split.

He'd have to learn to put up with her parents. The good news was her folks lived hours away.

The bad news was they had no boundaries where she was concerned.

Towel wrapped snugly about her body, she exited the bathroom in a cloud of steam, having enjoyed a little private time with his razor and her legs. She also made sure her garden was pruned.

She was feeling pretty good until she screamed, "Mom, Dad, what are you doing here?"

"We told you we would be back in the morning," rumbled her father. Dressed in khaki walking shorts and an eye-popping Hawaiian shirt, her father had taken a spot on the couch, his leg in the walking cast stretched before him.

As for Mom, she was dressed in pressed white slacks, a pastel-colored blouse, and hair that defied gravity with its poufy height. "You look a little tired, dear. Long night?"

Given how used to her mother she was, it would take more than a sly innuendo to embarrass Cynthia. "I'm fine, Mother." If by fine she meant sexually sated, kind of seeing a guy, and wondering if she was pregnant with a pair of tadpoles.

Daryl strolled out of the kitchen area, looking way more relaxed than a man should. "About time you got out of there. My mom's been waiting to meet you."

The morning seemed determined to make her blush.

"Your mom? Just let me get dressed and—" Yeah, the universe wasn't going to grant her the kindness of putting on underwear and a bra before meeting Daryl's mother.

There was no denying the woman who emerged from the kitchen was Daryl's mother. It wasn't just the tanned skin that gave it away, but the same dark gaze and straight nose. But where Daryl's chin was distinctly male, his mother's angled into a point, and she was tiny beside her son.

"Cyn, this is my mother, Luisa. Mama, I'd like you to meet Cynthia. She's um"—he paused and sent her an indecipherable look before shrugging and saying—"my girlfriend."

Dear God. Had he just publicly announced their status? Too late to take it back now. Her mother had heard and leaned forward in her seat. Some predators smelled blood in the air. Her mother smelled a wedding dress.

Luisa eyed her. "Does she cook?"

The question might not have been directed at her, but Cynthia answered it anyhow. "Yes. I can cook. Bake. As well as balance a checkbook, plan a dinner party for twelve, and wear heels while doing it." Her mother had insisted Cynthia learn certain skills growing up. Some like culinary creations she did well with. Others that involved needle and thread... Best not spoken of.

"Family is important?"

Her mom got in on the conversation. "Very. My Thea is a good girl. Never any problems with her."

The two women shared a nod, and Cynthia could already feel the tight strings of a corset as her mother plotted to reproduce the nightmare of her sweet sixteen dress shopping, but on a grander scale.

In that moment, Cynthia totally felt like a coyote and

was only missing a sign that said "help" as she tumbled off a cliff.

"Excellent. My Daryl needs a good woman to keep him in line. Don't forget, *gatito*, we are having dinner on Thursday. Bring your girlfriend." Daryl's mother paused at the door. "You and your husband should come, too." *You* being Cynthia's mother.

"We'd be delighted." Her mom beamed, a smile that was entirely too wide and happy. "Since I can see you're busy here, baby girl, we'll just take off. Daryl says you're meeting some friends to look for Aria's last whereabouts. But we'll be helping, too. Your father, being a car guy, is going to check out the junkyard just outside of town to see if Aria's motorcycle is there. Don't get into too much trouble."

"How about not any at all," grumbled her dad as he followed her mom out the door.

With the quiet *snick* of the door engaging, they were once again alone.

Blink. A few breaths.

No one came barging in, and Daryl still stood across the room looking entirely too calm.

Not acceptable. He should be as frazzled as her hair.

She dropped the towel. He spat out coffee.

"Could you warn me if you're going to do that?"

"No." She didn't even pretend to think about it. "What was all that about with your mom?" Although she feared she knew. *Looks like my mom isn't the only match-maker. We are so screwed.*

He shrugged. "Don't look at me. I came out of the bathroom as my mom was frying the bacon."

"There's bacon?" She didn't quite run to the kitchen, but it was close.

"Then while my mother whipped out some pancakes, your parents just walked in like they owned the place."

"Yeah, Daddy's not big on knocking. Or visiting people. He must like you." She beamed at him, a smile somewhat ruined by her chewing on a strip of pure pork heaven.

She plopped herself onto a bar stool and snagged a pancake with a fork from the platter stacked high with them, smothered it in butter and syrup, then moaned as she ate it, interspersing sweet bites with crunchy, salty bacon.

Fingers snapped in front of her nose. "Are you listening to me?"

"Um, can I lie and say yes?" She batted her lashes and wondered if he would get offended if she stole the last piece of bacon.

Screw it. She wanted it. He could spank her for it later.

Instead of the palm of his hand on her ass, she got a rundown of their battle plan. She straightened in her seat.

"Wes and Caleb are going to check some of the nearby campgrounds for signs of Aria."

"But Aria doesn't camp."

"That may be, but just in case, they're going to look."

"And what are we doing?" Although, whatever they did, she doubted it would rival the sex they'd had the previous night.

161

"We are going to be joined by Constantine to search the three motels in town."

"Why do we need his help? Wouldn't it make more sense to split up?"

"Given the attacks on us, not really."

Good point and a sobering one. While Cynthia was worried about dealing with her matchmaking mother—and now Daryl's, too—she couldn't forget that, despite Aria's call, there was something that smelled in Bitten Point, and it wasn't the swamp gases.

"Will the motels give us information on Aria? I thought there were some privacy laws against that."

"Yeah, but nothing a little nudge or a twenty won't fix, especially if they're shifters. Once they find out it's about a missing girl, they'll cooperate."

Cooperation was all well and good, but that required something for the desk staff to relate. After hitting the three motels within the town to no avail, they even hit a few on the outskirts. Money did exchange hands a few times, but the answer still remained a big fat negative. No one had seen a petite girl on a motorcycle, or if they had, they lied about it.

"It makes no sense," Cynthia grumbled, squished against the passenger door of Constantine's pickup truck because Daryl, for some reason, insisted on taking the middle spot on the bench seat.

Apparently, getting to ride inside the cab was a privilege, as usually the passenger spot was reserved for Princess, Constantine's dog. Not for this trip. His large-eyed furball currently sat in the big man's lap.

Having treated her fair share of Chihuahuas as a vet,

Cynthia knew they were extremely loyal with the heart of a lion. Seriously, those pipsqueaks feared nothing, and she'd gotten her fair share of nips when giving needles to know.

"Maybe your friend didn't book a motel for the night but stayed with a friend," Constantine ventured.

Frustrated at their failure to find anything, Cynthia snapped, "Are you calling her a slut?"

"You tell me."

Daryl threw out an arm, and she hit it before she could dive across the seat. When it came to Aria, Cynthia was her fiercest defender. In Constantine's case, he relied on his little dog. Princess peeled back her gums and growled.

Cynthia growled back.

As for Daryl, he tried to turn a chuckle into a cough before saying, "I'm sure that's not what he meant."

The big man at the wheel shot her a brief glance. "No, I wasn't calling her a slut, but asking if Aria might have spent the night with someone is a legitimate question. I mean, we've been concentrating on retracing her last steps and finding out more about those creatures who attacked you and have gotten nowhere. So it's time to change tactics. The best clue we have right now is your missing friend. We need to know more about her time in Bitten Point before that last night in the bar, starting with where the hell she was staying. If none of the hotels and motels remember her, and you're sure she wouldn't camp, then where was she sleeping and showering?"

Constantine's calm logic extinguished the fire in her. Cynthia slumped onto the seat. "Sorry I went all gangster on you. Especially since you're only trying to help. I don't know where she was staying, but it is possible she spent the night with a guy. Aria's a bit of a free spirit." Aria had learned at a young age to have a live-for-the-moment attitude. She took her pleasures when and where she could.

"Except you said she wouldn't have hooked up with a guy without telling you." Daryl grabbed her hand and held it, giving it a comforting squeeze.

"She never has before. But what other explanation is there? She had to stay somewhere." Cynthia could have kicked herself for not knowing. It just never came up in their previous chats, and for some reason, while Aria might have pinged the night at the bar with her phone, she never checked off a hotel or motel. Only foolish single women traveling alone would give out those kinds of details.

"We are fucking idiots," exclaimed Constantine with a snap of his fingers. "What about the bed and breakfast by Sal's place? The one past those orchards."

"Bedbug Bites?" Daryl said. "I thought the broad running that place shut it down."

The skin on Cynthia's body crawled at the thought of nighttime critters munching away. "Hold on, Bedbug Bites? What the heck kind of name is that for a B&B? Who would stay there?"

"Not humans," Daryl replied with a grin. "I told you the town had its methods of keeping them away. But a shifter would know the truth and realize it was a friendly joint for our kind."

"If that's the case, then why didn't we check this place out?" she asked.

"Because it closed down years ago to the public after Mrs. Jones' son went missing during the first round of monster appearances."

"If it's no longer open, then what makes you think Aria might have stayed there?"

"Because it might not be as closed as we thought," Constantine answered. "Veronica, the lady that owns the place, might not be publicly advertising she's open, yet for someone who is supposed to be living there alone, she gets a lot of groceries delivered."

It begged the question of, "And how do you know this?"

"My brother's mate. Renny used to work at the grocery store and was the one bagging the items for delivery. She thought it was weird, but none of her business."

Weird indeed, enough that they had to check it out.

The drive to this last-ditch effort took them down a lonely side road, one with deep ruts that had her bouncing since Cynthia couldn't find the oh-poop handle on the door. Don't mock her strong language. Being gangster didn't mean she could resort to the fouler words others used. Her mother's voice was too strong for that. *"Don't make me get the soap."* Shudder.

The second time she flailed for purchase and accidently squashed Daryl in his manparts, he grunted, but then put a stop to her unintentional damage. He dragged her onto his lap and anchored his arms around her. They still bounced, but now she could claim it was rather fun, given her proximity to a certain hottie.

"Where is this place? The ninth circle of Hell?" she

grumbled as she almost bit her tongue when they hit a pothole determined to suck in the truck.

"It's right on the edge of the swamp," Daryl replied. "All this land belongs to Veronica Jones. Her husband's family got it generations ago, over fifty acres, if I remember correctly."

Fifty acres of untamed jungle, given the foliage encroached upon the road. If she heard any banjos, she might start begging to turn around. Damn her ex-boyfriend for making her watch *Deliverance* and *The Hills Have Eyes*.

One moment they were looking lost and about to become meat-fodder in a horror movie and the next they emerged onto a paved, cobblestone drive that wound around a grassy circle with a stone bird bath in the middle.

The chill and uneasiness in Cynthia's bones didn't leave at the sight of the grand plantation home, the likes of which weren't often seen in these parts.

Tall columns graced the front and flanked the wide single step up to the pair of carved wooden front doors.

The pale siding had seen whiter days, the green and black hue of time and mildew doing its best to recolor them. Windows gaped upon the drive, their reflective surface showing the green foliage of the wilderness that surrounded the cultivated parts of this space.

As they stepped from the truck, Daryl doing so with one arm around her waist, holding her aloft as he slid them out, she couldn't help but smell the lushness of the greenery.

And the acrid stench of... "Dogman was here!"

No mistaking the nose-wrinkling smell of wet dog in dire need of a bath. Just like there was no mistaking Aria's bike tucked under a tarp off to the side of the drive.

Cynthia pushed out of Daryl's arms and ran to the familiar black cover with the patches they'd crazy-glued to repair tears. She dropped to her knees and lifted it to peer under. A red frame with hand-painted white daisies met her view. "Aria's here. We found her."

"I wouldn't get too excited yet," Daryl cautioned.

Her excitement plummeted.

"Don't get that look. I'm just saying that her bike being here doesn't mean she is. For all we know, she was taken from here and they left her stuff behind."

Good point, but she still couldn't help a little elation that they'd finally found some clue that Aria was in the area.

The hours for the B&B were posted on an engraved plaque alongside the doors. Registration from one p.m. until nine daily.

That was what the sign said, and here they were, almost five p.m., yet the door would not budge when pulled.

Daryl rapped his fist against it and then stood back to wait. They all waited. However, the only signs of life were in the buzz of insects around them. The blood-thirsty suckers went after the city girl with evil intent. Cynthia needed to get away from them, say like inside a house with doors and windows bearing screens. A problem remained, though. The door was locked, and no one seemed inclined to answer.

"Maybe the front desk person went to the bath-room?" she ventured.

"And locked the door so no guests could get in?" Daryl snorted and shook his head. "The only way this wouldn't be open was if we were mistaken and this place isn't a B&B at all."

"But the sign says—"

"That sign is old and was probably never removed when she shut down."

She couldn't refute Daryl's logic, given the plaque appeared fairly tarnished.

"Something's not right." Constantine uttered the words while looking off in the distance. A frown creased his brow, and his body was tense.

No, something wasn't right, and she didn't mean just the state of her hair in this humidity. The whole place oozed of creepiness. She would know. She'd watched her fair share of horror movies, and the one thing they all taught was don't go into the spooky, abandoned house.

Her inner canine whined. *Danger.* Eyes watched. Menace lurked. She shouldn't let paranoia get the better of her. Or should she listen to common sense?

"Maybe we should leave." She tucked herself tighter to Daryl, and he put a reassuring arm around her, but it couldn't dispel the chill.

"What's wrong?"

"I don't know, but Constantine is right. I don't feel right about this place. Maybe we should call the cops and let them come check things out."

"But what about looking for Aria? She was obviously here."

"You said it. Was. Her bike's been parked there for a while." The intricate spider web in the wheel rim with its desiccated catches said so. "She's obviously not in there."

"Or she is, but can't get out," Daryl countered, playing devil's advocate.

"Hey, guys, do you see Princess?" Constantine asked.

"Not me," she replied.

"Me either."

Constantine craned to look around. "Princess! Where are you? Come to Daddy."

The incongruous appearance of the giant Constantine baby-talking his dog proved hard to ignore, and she bit her lip lest she snicker. It was a battle she didn't fight alone, given Daryl's snort.

A sharp bark lightened the expression on Constantine's face, and he moved quickly around to the side of the house. They found a decent-sized yard with taut vinyl strung from the house for about thirty feet to a tree that served as a post. Laundry flapped from it, some of the fabric hanging by only a single pin.

Bark. The sharp sound drew their attention to Princess. The small dog stood on a wooden stoop, pawing at a door. It had a window set into it, covered in a flower-patterned curtain.

Instead of rapping on the door, Constantine peered in.

"See anything?" Daryl asked.

"Nah. It's just some kind of mudroom with a washer and dryer. I am going to go inside to check it out," Constantine announced.

"Should we? I mean, isn't that breaking and entering?" Cynthia whispered. She couldn't have said why she kept her voice low, maybe to avoid disturbing spirits, or because if conspiring to commit a crime, she probably shouldn't shout about it.

"It's only break and enter if the door is locked." Daryl pointed at the splintered jamb. "Looks like we're not the first ones to want in."

The realization only increased the size of the knot in her stomach.

Don't go in!

Her wolf really, really thought it was a bad idea. Funny, Cynthia did, too, but to not follow meant staying outside. She cast a glance at the bordering swamp vegetation, most of it thick enough to hide any number of threats.

She clasped Daryl's hand tightly. She was sticking to his side and hoping they didn't run into anything dangerous, especially since she no longer had any needles. The supplies she'd brought had gotten toasted in the fire.

That won't be cheap to replace. But considering she'd escaped alive and unscathed, she was still ahead of the game.

Constantine put himself to the side of the door and, with one hand, pushed at it. It remained closed. It took a firm shove to swing it open.

She held her breath, her body tensed... Nothing jumped out.

Princess showed no fear and scampered over the sill. The big guy slid through next, Daryl at his heels, and since she held his hand, Cynthia followed as well, a choice she regretted with her first step into the house.

Ugh, Cynthia thought. *Ooh, dead thing,* was her wolf's addition. Sometimes, having a wild animal with different ideas about good and bad provided an interesting mindset.

While her nose wrinkled at the stench of something wrong, and she didn't mean just wet-dog wrong, her wolf wanted her to follow the smell that made her gag.

Don't puke.

"What is that smell?" she gasped, and why was it so hot? It seemed the air conditioning in the place wasn't working, the indoors just as hot and humid as the outside. Hotter perhaps even.

"AC is off. Actually, I think the whole power to this place is." Constantine flicked the pair of switches by the door, but the overhead light remained dark.

As they slipped from the mudroom into the kitchen, the smell grew stronger. Cynthia filtered some of it by having her T-shirt pulled up over her nose. She glanced around, noting the flies that buzzed around a pile of dirty dishes in the sink. Fruit in a bowl, barely recognizable, made a great science experiment.

It seemed someone had left without cleaning first.

In here there was more evidence something had happened, and not recently, given the fridge, when opened, showed moldy food. The power had obviously been gone for some time.

"Where should we check first?" Daryl asked.

Other than the mudroom, there were two options in the kitchen. One archway led to the dining room, the other to the hall. She could spot the rails on a staircase leading to a second level.

"Let's check the registration desk first."

Cynthia wanted to vote for the dining room. She could tell the stench was stronger out in the hall. She could almost see the miasma of wrongness in the air.

Death, her wolf advised.

Death and decay, and the culprit was the body they located on the floor behind the front desk.

Cynthia slapped a hand over her mouth, but it wasn't enough. While she could handle sewing wounds and minor operations and even blood, what she saw on the floor? That sent her running to puke outside.

Chapter 18

Daryl's T-shirt of the day: *"I'm a ray of fucking sunshine."*

INSTEAD OF CHASING AFTER CYN, who was looking to fertilize nature with her breakfast, he yelled after her. "Don't go far from the house and keep Princess with you."

Cyn wasn't the only delicate lady in need of fresh air. Daryl kind of wanted to join them. However, outside wasn't where the clues were.

As for letting her out of his sight? The dogman scent trace wasn't recent, just like this body. Judging by the lilac-colored pants and matching blouse, the corpse was probably what remained of poor Mrs. Jones.

"Looks like an animal got to her," Constantine observed without touching the body.

"Animal, or one of our new friends?" The stench of decay proved too strong to pinpoint if it was the dogman or dinoman that got to her, yet given he'd not scented anything reptilian, he was going to lean toward the canine.

"We should search the house. See if there are any more victims."

"Think we might find the guy who did this?"

Constantine shook his head. "This wasn't done by no guy. Only a monster could do something like this."

True. "Should we stick together or split up?"

"Want me to hold your hand, too?" Constantine snickered.

"Fuck off," was Daryl's reply. "It's a valid question, given those dudes are tough as nails."

"If you run into one, then let out a scream."

"Excuse me, but don't you mean bellow in a manly fashion?" Daryl retorted.

A snort left Constantine. "I'll check out the main floor." His friend stalked into the living room area.

"I take it I'm checking the bedrooms then," Daryl muttered, not that anyone heard. With a quick peek out the window, and spotting Cyn pacing, her expression pale, Daryl went looking for more bodies—and really hoped he didn't find a particular one.

While Cynthia was holding it together pretty well, given her friend's strange disappearance, he knew finding Aria dead would crush her.

He couldn't allow that to happen. *I care too much about her to see her hurt.*

Gag. And, no, it wasn't because of a hairball. He was

thinking and feeling things he'd never imagined for a woman, and it came without effort or even thought. It was all so damned freaky, but he couldn't stop it, nor did he want to.

I want Cyn in my life. Even more, he wanted her happy.

The fact that the decaying smell receded as he tread carefully upstairs proved somewhat reassuring. The line of closed doors? Not so much.

When the first knob he tried wouldn't cooperate, he didn't think twice. He lifted a booted foot and kicked.

Bang!

So much for keeping their presence secret. Nothing came charging out of the other closed doors, although Constantine did yell, "Do you need Princess to save you?"

"I hope she gives you fleas," he hollered back. The joking served to ease some of his tension, but he truly breathed a sigh of relief when he realized the room he'd entered might have feminine belongings scattered, but no body.

But that doesn't mean they're Aria's.

After a quick peek in the closet and attached bath-room—both empty—he headed back into the hall. Three more doors to go.

The next one he kicked proved empty, the bed neatly made, the bathroom empty of toiletries. Not so for the next two. The first one, while tidy, did have a suitcase in the closet and clothes neatly hung. The other room was more of a disaster with men's apparel strewn all over, not out of violence but more a slovenly nature.

With their discovery, he'd go out on a limb and wager the first room belonged to Aria, a guest of this B&B, who wasn't alone in being missing. What happened to the other two occupants?

Utterly strange, yet he didn't pause to check it out further, not when he realized there was still a third floor. The spiral steps at the end of the hall wound upwards, but he couldn't see what lay above him. He emerged onto a small landing lit by a porthole window set in the side of the house. The paneled door didn't impede him. A swift kick took care of it.

The entire third floor, which might have begun as an attic, had been transformed into an apartment. The open area contained a living room with a small kitchen area. On one side, he found a bedroom, the scent of lilacs strong. The faded quilt on the bed reminded him of the one his mother kept in the linen closet because her grandma had made it. The dresser, made of carved wood, held an array of crystal bottles, perfume in some. Others seemed to hold only colored water. Even though he smelled nothing in here that seemed out of place, he checked the closet.

Nothing. So he headed to the other side where the first door yielded a bathroom. Nothing strange there.

But the next room proved sad. Pictures of a boy, awkward-looking with a stiff smile, lined the walls, the progression in age easy to follow. There was a twin-sized bed in here, covered in a navy blue comforter. Figurines —*Star Wars* and wrestlers and other comic book icons— were spread across the dresser and the two shelves hung on the wall.

A bedroom shrine to the son Mrs. Jones had lost.

He backed out and shut the door. No use in stirring up ghosts.

As he strode to the large diamond-shaped window, intent on peeking outside—*oh admit it, you want to check on Cyn*—he peered around Mrs. Jones' living space. Certain details popped out at him such as the fact that it was decked out in posh furniture, the leather on the couches real and buttery soft. Hung on the wall he noted a television to make even the biggest man drool. The carpet underfoot proved thick and lush—no cheap Berber here—just like the appliances gleamed with newness. Daryl had to wonder how big her husband's life insurance policy was because there was no freaking way this remote bed and breakfast brought in the kind of money needed for luxury at this level. If it did, then he was in the wrong business.

Nothing stood out in this space, apart from the largesse, so he returned to the second floor and stepped in the room he'd pegged as Aria's.

Cyn stood at the foot of the brass railed bed, hugging a bright scarf to her chest, her eyes bright with tears. "These are Aria's things."

He moved close enough to wrap an arm around her, pulling her close to his body. "We'll find her."

"But will she be alive or like that—that—" She couldn't say it, and he didn't even want her to think it.

He pressed her face into his shoulder, letting the fabric of his shirt absorb her tears. Soothing noises hummed from him as he stroked her back until, with a sniffle, she lifted her face.

"I'm sorry," she hiccupped.

"Don't be sorry for caring. You've done great so far. I mean, look at everything that's happened to you. First, you're a drugging kidnapper, then a pillow-smashing thug, then a bumper car survivor. And let's not forget femme fatale."

She snorted, the sound watery, but already getting some of her spirit back. "Okay, that was stretching it. And you forgot coward. I totally tossed my cookies downstairs."

"But stopped to rinse your mouth," he noted with a quirk of his lips.

Her nose wrinkled. "I did, and I popped a mint. I saw them in a jar on the counter. Oh God. I just ate a dead person's candy."

Before the tears could start again, he said quickly, "Sniff. Tell me what you get."

"I can't. My nose is stuffy."

However, the excuse gave her a chance to collect herself, and he really wondered how bad he had it for Cyn, given she honked her nose loud and hard, but he thought she was still the cutest damned thing he'd ever seen.

Shoot me now.

It was with their asses in the air, and their snoots to the ground, that Constantine found them.

"Pete and a few deputies are on their way. They're not announcing it on the airwaves because they want to check the scene first in case there's something we need to hide about our kind."

"Of course he's not announcing it," Daryl grumbled,

trying not to sneeze at the dust that hadn't seen a vacuum in a while. "Announcing it might let people know there's a killer amongst us." It still bugged him that their own sheriff was going along with the secrecy.

"I don't smell the dog guy in here," Cyn announced, sitting back on her haunches.

Daryl leaned on his heels as well and frowned at the room. "I don't either, yet there's something here. Something that doesn't belong."

"Wasn't this the shirt she was wearing in the picture?" Constantine said, holding aloft a crimson top and touching his nose to it.

Cyn snatched it. "Yes, and there's that chunky pendent she wore with it. So she did come back here that night."

But what happened to her next?

Chapter 19

Cynthia: So I came across a dead
      body today.
Mom: Need help burying it?

SINCE DARYL and Constantine seemed determined to investigate every fiber in that B&B bedroom, Cynthia left, but descended via the rear steps. The boys had given the house an all-clear, the dogman stench restricted to the outdoors it seemed, and old at that.

In the distance, she could hear the sound of car engines and doors slamming, the sign chaos would soon descend in the form of cops.

Cops here to investigate the body in the front hall, a body that wasn't Aria's, thank goodness.

But it could have been. Whatever attacked the owner could have easily gone after other guests.

Daryl said it was a good sign they'd not found any signs of violence against Aria. Personally, Cynthia thought that was worse. It meant whatever came for her best friend didn't give her warning or time to defend herself.

According to Aria's phone call, she lived, but for what purpose? She'd heard Daryl and his buddies toss around the idea of shifter experimentation, and with the chief of police insisting the SHC knew what was happening and wished to turn a blind eye, she had to wonder if those suppositions were in fact true.

Was someone taking shifters from Bitten Point and playing God with them?

Shiver.

Surely not. The Shifter High Council would never stand for that. Would they?

The rear staircase led to an open area of sorts at the back of the house. On one side, a hallway stretched, and the faint whiff of decomposition made her tummy clench.

Not going that way.

On the other side was another wide arch leading to a formal dining room, done old-school style with vintage crown molding and white wainscoting, offset by dark and gleaming floor and window trim. The walls above the chair rail wall were hung with rose-patterned wallpaper, somewhat faded, yet a perfect look for a home of this style.

Off the dining area was a room that could only be termed a parlor with its blue velvet-covered chairs held aloft on spindly legs. Wooden curio cabinets with glass shelves were packed with eggs, all kinds of Faberge type eggs, in a rainbow of colors.

She heard a commotion of voices as the cavalry arrived, but she had no interest in answering their questions yet. Leave that to Daryl and Constantine.

The French doors to the garden beckoned, and she stepped out of them, breathing deep of the air, redolent with the smell of fresh flowers with an undertone of bayou. Like many places in Bitten Point, this home's property skirted the edges, the wildness of the swamp vegetation providing an interesting contrast with the more cultured and planned elegance of the garden.

A stone bench by a pond only a few paces from the door beckoned. She sat and let her fingers trail in the water, melancholy tugging at her spirit. To think they'd finally found a clue about Aria's last moments and immediately hit another roadblock when no true path to her friend emerged.

Why couldn't we have found a map or some coordinates that said Aria is here?

Then again, once she found her friend, she'd have no reason to stay.

Ahem.

Okay, so she did have a reason—Daryl, but she still wasn't too sure what he saw in their future.

If our mothers have their way, we'll be married before the end of the next week. But it wasn't up to their parents to decide, although it would help if they could.

It was pretty obvious Daryl had not meant to mark her. Romantic as it was that he'd lost control, she knew they couldn't base a future on a lapse of reason, a moment of passion. She was just as guilty of it as he was.

Lust shouldn't decide whom a person spent the rest of their life with.

Is lust all we have?

What about her enjoyment of his presence? Their love of onion rings. The way he made her feel.

But he doesn't know our secret.

Her wolf was so worried, yet Cynthia could state with a fair measure of confidence that she didn't think Daryl was the type to care about a defect on her part.

"It's not that bad," she muttered aloud.

As if her wolf listened. She seemed perfectly content to hide within.

Some people's inner beast proved aggressive, and strong-minded, insisting on being a part of all the decisions and getting their fair share of time outside the human skin.

Not Cynthia's wolf. Her wolf was more than happy to let Cynthia stay in charge. Yet Cynthia in charge didn't mean her wolf didn't look out for her.

Danger.

The sudden stillness in the bayou caught her attention. Her head perked, and she was pretty sure her ears did, too, even if they couldn't move in this shape.

The hush that fell was unnatural. The swamp was never quiet, not when its residents always made noise. Yet something had silenced them. A predator walked nearby.

It belatedly occurred to Cynthia that perhaps sitting out here wasn't the wisest course, all alone in a place where murder and other nefarious acts had taken place. Never mind there were cops out front as well as Daryl and Constantine nearby. Could they reach her in time should something attack?

Eep.

Darting glances around her, Cynthia scurried back to the safety of the house, closing the French doors and locking them. Silly, really, given a determined person—or creature—would easily smash through the glass.

Funny how, a few days ago, these types of thoughts would have never crossed her mind. Now, though, she saw danger everywhere. Sometimes in plain sight.

Her mouth opened as she watched the lizard man with the leathery wings step from the shadows of a willow tree on the edge of the property. His gaze locked with hers, and he took a step forward. She took one back.

A part of her wanted to scream. Yell. Do something.

Daryl and so many other people were only steps away, but if she called for help, the lizard thing would take off, and despite his appearance, she wasn't entirely sure he intended to hurt.

Still, a girl couldn't be too careful. She whirled for just a second, eyes scanning the parlor for something to use as a weapon. The brass figurine on the mantel for the fireplace looked as if it might have some weight. She tugged it, but instead of coming free, it bent on a hinge.

But that wasn't the most startling thing.

With only the faintest of creaks, the façade for the fireplace slid to the side. Instant wet-dog smell wafted out, but of more interest, she recognized Aria's worn pink bunny slipper on the inside of the cavity. She hesitated before the opening, the brave part of her insisting she go looking for her friend. The smart part of her consciousness smacked her brain and told her to go get Daryl.

Before she could turn around, something clocked her from behind!

Chapter 20

Constantine's shirt, a present from Daryl: *"If my Chihuahua doesn't like you, then neither will I."*

DARYL PEEKED from the bedroom window, watching Cyn in the garden. Her fingers trailed in the pond water covered in a layer of lily pads. A part of him wanted to shout at her to come inside. Something agitated his feline. It paced his mind, insisting she put herself in danger by sitting out there alone.

Then again, walls hadn't saved the old woman who now lay dead behind the counter, nor had it protected Aria, it appeared, or the other occupants whose dusty articles remained scattered and forgotten.

What happened here?

As a guy who'd tracked his fair share of prey in the woods surrounding the bayou, Daryl knew how to piece together what happened from scent.

Certain emotions and acts held a particular flavor to them. Violence had a flavor, sharp and hair-raising. Fear was a sour and acrid stench. Blood, of course, had its own scent, coppery and meaty at the same time.

None of those were in this room, yet Aria must have disappeared from it or nearby because on the dresser was her purse and, inside it, her wallet and some cash.

As Daryl stared from the window, he stroked the short beard on his chin, watching Cyn and wondering if perhaps with the danger floating around he should send her away. Send her somewhere safe, somewhere with no abnormal dogmen or dinomen or attempts to kill or, as Cyn appeared convinced, of things trying to kidnap her.

With her friend missing, though, would Cyn leave? She possessed a delightful stubbornness, along with a love and loyalty for her friend. But the harder they looked, the more dire things became.

And the more convoluted.

Look at the wealth of clues in this B&B alone. Several disappearances, none reported by the owner of the house —*perhaps because she was involved?*

Could knowledge be the reason Mrs. Jones had died? A loose end snipped before it could spill any secrets?

Despite the attempts to wipe their tracks, we're getting closer. Daryl could sense it, almost smell it with that sixth sense predators had when they were closing in on their target. When they did get in sight, he was coiled and ready to pounce.

Something rotten was preying on Bitten Point, going after the unknown and vulnerable. It had to stop. *I will make it stop.*

Movement outside the window grabbed his attention. Cyn rose and moved away from the pond to scurry inside. Had she heard or seen something?

The edges of the bayou lined the cleared yard, the stretching tendrils of the swamp looking to take back what it had lost.

It didn't take Daryl long to spot the lizard creature, stepping from the filmy tendrils of the tree. The thing stood and stared in the direction Cyn had gone. Then it lifted its head and caught Daryl's gaze immediately.

Nothing else was done. No rude gestures or implied body language. The dinoman didn't snarl or howl or blow fucking fire or whatever his weird kind did.

He just stood staring, and in that moment, Daryl wondered at its story. How did it become what it was? Because Daryl was now certain there was something unnatural, something forced or created, to make the two creatures they'd encountered the way they were.

The fading sunlight glinted off metal around the creature's neck, that odd collar that Cyn argued controlled their actions.

The lizard man, as if sensing his curiosity, reached a hand to grasp at the collar. Tugged it. Roared.

Then roared in Daryl's direction before loping into the vegetation bordering the yard. Only then did it occur to Daryl that he should have gone after it or at least told Constantine to while he tried to keep its attention.

The thing was a monster. It needed to be stopped.

The sound of thumping feet announced the arrival of the sheriff and a deputy. He peeked in and sniffed. "Any other bodies up here?"

"Nope, but the girl this room belonged to is missing."

"It happens," Pete replied. "Look at my son. One day, he's working at Bittech, the next he takes off, won't tell me where he's gone, and only calls to say he's doing great."

"At least your son is calling."

"I heard your lady got a call, too. So what makes you think this girl is missing?"

"I'd say the dead body downstairs proves something is going on."

"Looks like a simple robbery to me." Pete tucked his thumbs into his belt loops.

"Wouldn't shit have to be taken for it to be theft?" he pointed out.

"We don't know for sure what's gone yet. Could be they were after the old lady's cash."

"Or someone is trying to cover their traces."

A grimace wrinkled the sheriff's face. "Watch that you don't let paranoia get to you, boy. It's a wily creature that sinks its claws in and looks for ways to feed itself. While conspiracy theories are fun, most times, the simplest answer is the truth."

Daryl might put more stock in Pete's attempts to allay his fears, except he'd now seen too much in the past few days. He'd experienced things that really hit close to home, like when his sister disappeared for a little bit a few weeks back. What about the fact that Cyn almost got killed? He counted himself damned lucky she'd emerged unscathed.

Our mate needs protecting.

Gack. And, no, that wasn't a hairball that just about made him choke. It was the realization that he cared so much about Cyn. Cared.

Oh hell. No matter how many times he wanted to deny it, he was falling for Cyn. The bite wasn't an accident. He wanted her to wear his mark to show the world she was his.

Although, if I wanted it to show, perhaps I should have put it in a different spot. In order for someone to see it, she'd have to take off her pants.

Hell no. The only person she would strip for was him —even if the money was ridiculously good. Daryl wasn't afraid to apply a double standard to his girlfriend. It seemed he had jealousy issues he'd never known existed. Coveting Cyn. It sounded fucking dirty and fucking great.

The mental cursing and somewhat dirty thoughts went a long way to helping him deal with his epiphany and Pete's inane assertions that there was nothing untoward happening.

The sheriff and Constantine had their heads together talking, but mostly about the basics they'd discovered.

"I should go check on Cyn."

Yes, we should. Our mate needs us.

Cool it, he told his inner feline. *Admitting that I want her in my life doesn't mean I'm about to super glue myself to her side. She is a grown woman. I can't smother her all the time.*

We should cover her at night. Naked.

Deal.

Some people might find his mental bargaining with his cat odd, except Daryl was of the mind that sharing a body meant sharing decisions, compromising. Some people let themselves completely control the beast, going so far even as to repress it. His friend Caleb had done that for a long time, fighting his inner crocodile, convinced the cold-blooded reptile inside him was evil.

Caleb learned that balance was needed, something that Daryl had known all along.

With his determination that Cyn would be fine on her own—she was, after all, in a house now crawling with officers of the law, and not only were they all armed, they were shifters as well—he decided to check out those other rooms again, especially once he noted that Constantine and Pete had left the room to explore. He trailed behind, ignoring his panther pacing in his mind. Running downstairs to check on Cyn would wait.

The room a few feet down the hall held the interest of Constantine and Pete. They sifted through the stuff in the room, with the sheriff actually locating a wallet on the nightstand.

"The driver's license is for one Jeffrey Moore. He's from New England, according to this."

"But what was he doing here?" Constantine asked.

It was Daryl who noted the jacket hanging on the back of the chair, but more importantly, the name badge pinned to it.

"He's got a Bittech Employee card." Daryl held it up. "I'll have to call Wes and see what he knows about him."

As head security guard, Wes had access to employee records and had suspected, for a while, the company of underhanded dealings. The CEO, who happened to be Daryl's sister's husband, told Wes that everything they were doing was SHC approved. More and more, Daryl wondered if their blind acceptance of that was foolish. The SHC was only as good as the people ruling it.

"Here's his laptop." Constantine pulled it from a case and put it on the bed.

The laptop booted as soon as the power button was held down. However, the log-in screen stumped them, and less than a minute later, the screen went black as the laptop died.

"I guess Mr. Jeffrey Moore is keeping his secrets."

"For now. I'll take a peek at it," Constantine offered. "I might be able to find something."

Pete scrubbed a hand over his jowls, suddenly looking every one of his fifty-three years. "Do that, but keep it on the down low. Report only to me what you find. We don't want to make you a target."

"What happened to us maybe being paranoid?" Daryl couldn't resist the jibe.

Pete's lips pressed tight together. "I'm still hoping there's a rational explanation for all this."

"Other than the obvious that they were taken?" The snort went well with his arched brow. "I don't know why you keep covering it up."

"I told you, the SHC—"

"Fuck the SHC. There are people disappearing and being murdered. *Murdered.*" Daryl growled as he took a step forward. "So be a man, be an officer of the law, and do your fucking job. Protect the fucking people of this town. Or, if you can't do that, then at least make an attempt to do what's fucking right."

For a moment, Pete's face hardened, and Daryl braced for a punch. Surely the bigger, older man wouldn't let Daryl ream him like that, even if well deserved.

Instead, the lines in Pete's face sagged, along with his shoulders. "I know you're right. There is something wrong. Problem is, being right isn't simple... Or safe."

A voice called out from the hall. "Sir. We've cleared the main floor and swept the grounds."

"Did you find anyone else?"

Chet poked his head in the door, his freckled cheeks pale. The body wasn't something any one of them took lightly. "No more bodies, if that's what you're asking."

"What about suspects?"

"Negative. While we came across a few scents, there is no one but the men we came with and these two on the premises."

"And Cynthia," Daryl added.

Chet frowned. "Is that who's in the main hall? That body is still there."

"Body? I'm not talking about a corpse. I'm talking about Cyn, the girl you caught me with the other night. About chin-high, cocoa skin, and smelling of wolf."

Even before the Chet shook his head, Daryl was moving. He trampled down the stairs, taking them two and three at a time, doing more vaulting than stepping. On the main level, he took a moment to smell the air, paying little attention to the pair of guys taking pictures of the body.

Given they couldn't hide a murder, they treated it like a crime scene, bagging and tagging items while, at the same time, removing or wiping clean any evidence of this being a less-than-human crime. Actually, in this case, they would spin it as a wild animal attack. Yet that weak explanation wouldn't work with the abandoned items found on the second floor.

Hard to hide three disappearances in one place.

Maybe four.

No. Don't think that way. But he couldn't help a spurt of anxiety as he noted Cyn wasn't in the main hall or out front with the cop cars. Nor did he locate her in the kitchen, the comfortable living room, or the dining room. However, in the last, he did at least catch a hint of her scent. He followed it, ignoring its trail to the French doors and, instead, approached the fireplace.

He sniffed long and deep. There was Cyn, still smelling of his soap. Then, another scent he recognized, but didn't. It tickled with familiarity.

It was Constantine who had caught up to Daryl that nailed it for him. "That's the same smell that came from that guy's room."

"But I thought the theory was he was missing. This scent is fresh." It also didn't seem to move from this room.

Following his nose, and trying not to think of that ditty from the Froot Loops commercial, he went to the patio doors, grasping the fabric of the hanging drape and bringing it to his face. "He hid in the curtains. Then"—Daryl dropped the material and pivoted to face the fireplace—"he crept out while Cyn was standing here." Standing before the mantel, Daryl frowned. "And then it's like they both disappeared."

"First we have dinoman and dogman. Don't tell me just found invisi-man."

A frown pulled Daryl's brows together. "This isn't fucking funny, dude. Cyn is missing."

"I wasn't being funny. I mean, come on. Given what we've seen, can you really deny the possibility?"

"Yeah, I will, because invisibility as a trait could happen. All it would take was a very chameleon-like method of blending into the background, but at the same time, background blending wouldn't hide scent."

"Says you. Science can—"

"Kiss my ass," Daryl retorted. "She did not vanish into thin air with some dude." It wasn't even something he could contemplate, and besides, his cat was poking him again, and given it was right about Cyn needing him —*don't you fucking smirk at me, kitty*—he wasn't about to ignore it again.

"Fine then. If you don't think invisi-dude took her, then where did she go?" Constantine gestured to the room. "I might not have your developed sense of smell, but I have eyes, and they don't see her in this room. Or any of the rooms in this house unless she's hiding."

Grr. Ruff.

During their discussion, Princess had entered the room with its impractical chairs and other dainty items. She sniffed at the fireplace, tiny black nose pressed to the floor.

Grr. Ruff. She made noise again and pawed at the wall.

"Do you have to tinkle?" Constantine asked his dog.

If a dog could give a disgusted look, Princess did. Very deliberately, she turned from Constantine and scratched the wall. Then she turned just her head to shoot her owner an expectant look.

"She thinks there's something there." Impossible given the dining room was on the other side of that wall.

Daryl took the few strides needed to peek through the archway. Big wooden table, straight-backed chairs, a chandelier. No Cyn. Just a plain dining room...that was narrower than the room he'd just come from.

A frown pulled at his features. He strode quickly through to the kitchen, a kitchen the same size as the back room.

An idea glimmered, and he returned to the sitting room, more specifically the fireplace. He crouched down to peek at the edges.

Princess gave him her first approving look ever, and it occurred to Daryl that maybe the dog was kind of cute.

"What are you looking for?" Constantine asked.

"Seams. See them?" Daryl traced the line up the jut of stone then across the mantel. His hand brushed a statue, which wobbled.

It didn't fall, but was it him, or did the fireplace tremble?

He knocked the statue over, and it stayed flopped as the fireplace shifted to the side, revealing a dark entrance.

"I'll be damned. Secret passage." Every young boy's dream.

A whiff of mildew and dust wafted but, of more interest was a familiar scent. "Cyn and that fellow went this way."

"It looks like it goes down," Constantine observed, sticking his head in. "I wonder if this links to the tunnels I hear they built."

"What tunnels?"

"My grandfather told me about them when I was a kid. Rumor has it pirate smugglers built tunnels under the bayou, linking them to an oceanside cove."

"Surely they would have caved by now."

Constantine shrugged. "Maybe, except rumor also has it they were used back in the eighties and nineties to move drugs."

"That's insane. How the hell would we not know about tunnels under the town?" Daryl prided himself on being a smart guy, or at least an observant one. It burned he didn't know about this possibility.

"No one knows, for the same reason humans don't know we're right under their nose. A well-crafted lie is sometimes easier to believe than the truth. And let's be honest, we might be half-beast, but even we can't know about everything that's going on. The swamp is too big, and we are too few."

"And not everyone gives a shit." Just like some people could be bought. Greed wasn't just a human failing.

Daryl began to strip out of his clothes just as Constantine turned around. "What the hell, dude?"

"I'm going after Cyn. Since neither of us has a gun, I'd rather be prepared to fight."

"We could ask the cops for help," Constantine suggested.

No way could Daryl have held in his snicker.

Constantine joined him. "Okay, so we don't want to share the fun. I'm cool with that, but unlike you, I am going to keep my clothes on and rely on these two things." A big fist met the palm of his other big hand. When it came to fisticuffs, Constantine proved deadly and very light on his feet, something most of his opponents didn't expect. They had a chance to regret their mistake usually for about two seconds before Constantine knocked them out.

Daryl loved the money he collected on those wagers.

The change from smooth skin and two legs to four tipped in paws with claws wasn't a whoosh and a blink-of-the-eye procedure. It didn't take long—nature's way of ensuring they weren't vulnerable in between shapes—but the rapidity of an entire body changing its cellular structure to a new shape was not exactly pain free.

However, the pain proved fleeting, the excruciating agony in but a few blinks of the eye that was quickly forgotten in the thrill of wearing his other shape.

As his panther, all of his senses were sharper. The world might come to him in a slightly different way, yet there was nothing strange about it. He understood what the different shades he perceived meant, from the air currents to the heat, to the sharpness that allowed him to discern even the faintest of patterns in sifted dust.

As he padded into the hidden entrance, he did not yet bother to lower his nose to smell. No need. The trail practically blazed before him.

With each step, his cold fury grew. Felines might prove disdainful by nature. They might seem like good time tomcats with no cares, but that just hid the cold predator within. Cats were territorial, and if there was one thing Daryl thought of as his, that was Cyn.

She's my mate. And she needed him.

He just hoped he found her in time.

Chapter 21

Cynthia: So a psychopath knocked me
out and chained me to a wall.
Mom: Does this mean you're going to be
later for dinner?

REGAINING consciousness with a throbbing head was
either a sign she'd had a really, really good time and drank a
few too many or, in this case, seeing as how she was chained
to a ring hammered into a cement wall, really, really bad.

Cynthia groaned as she pushed herself to a seated
position, all she could manage given the circumstances.
The metal rattle of the handcuff on her wrist kept her on
a short leash. Her captive status also seemed a clear indi-
cator someone wanted her to stay put. Given Cynthia

counted herself a normal woman with normal reactions, she didn't take it nicely, or quietly.

"Let me go! Help! Someone, save me. Help!"

Scream as she might, no one came. No matter how she abused her vocal cords, no one answered. All she could hear was the steady *drip drip drip* of water.

Bummer—and it gave her quite the urge to pee. No urinating would happen until she got loose, though. She tugged at the metal bracelet holding her prisoner, heaving and ho-ing, to no avail. Even propping her feet on the wall and pulling with all her weight didn't budge the ring firmly embedded in the wall. It did, however, dig the metal into her wrists, and in turn, her inability to free herself depressed her.

It's useless.

Breaking free using brute force wouldn't happen. She slumped, with her back resting against the cold, dank wall. Such a barren and icky place. How had she gotten here?

One minute she'd peeked in a secret passage, and the next, she'd woken here with a throbbing head. Where was here, though, and how long had she been unconscious?

Without a watch or a phone, she couldn't tell how much time had passed. This place had no window to gauge the position of the sun. For all she knew, bare minutes or hours could have elapsed. One thing she could probably count on was that the longer she remained here, the more likely it was that whoever chained her would return. It didn't take a refined sense of smell to note the strong stench of a dog left out in the damp.

Even more disturbing was the hint of the same type of meaty decay she smelled at the B&B. *Please don't tell me there's a body in here.* The feeble light from the one dangling bulb didn't exactly illuminate the shadowy corners piled with moldy boxes and crates.

The skitter of tiny feet didn't reassure. Where there scampered one rat, more surely followed.

We have to get out of here! Her wolf's insistence only served to heighten her own anxiety. Surely there must be something she'd missed, some way to escape. She'd already tried brute force and failed. What of a tool, an item she could use to pry at the metal links?

A crowbar would be perfect.

Her rude kidnapper, however, had failed to provide anything she could use within reach, or so she discovered when she visually catalogued every inch of the space. A very strange place.

It resembled a bomb bunker with concrete walls, sturdy shelving bolted to it, and metal cans, rusted on the edges, the labels long since molded into obscurity. The corners held leaning piles of boxes, most of them collapsed and spilling moldy straw. Packing material before those popcorn Styrofoam pieces came along. Whatever the room's use, it seemed as if it had been abandoned a long while ago.

Which really doesn't bode well for rescue.

Clink. Cynthia tugged again at her manacles and then glared at the cuff ringing her wrist. If only she could shrink her hand.

Hold on. She eyed her body—her very human body. There was a way to make her wrist smaller.

Stripping down wasn't easy one-handed and crouched on the floor. It also proved chilly in this dark place, lit by only a single light bulb flickering from the ceiling. How nice of her kidnapper to leave her light. It would have been nicer if he'd left her alone.

With her arm bound, Cynthia could only partially remove her shirt, but with it hanging off her shackled arm, she didn't fear getting caught in the fabric. Nothing more rookie than getting bound in clothes during a shift. It had happened during her teenage years when she found herself self-conscious about stripping down on a full moon for a run with others.

As naked as she was getting, she sucked in a deep breath. *Ready?* She couldn't have said if she aimed the query at herself or her wolf. Teeth gritted tight, she allowed the change to happen. It drew a sharp cry from her. Expecting the pain never made it any easier. However, much like childbirth—or so her mother claimed —the pain soon faded, leaving behind only the unpleasant memory.

In her four-legged form, her wolf took the driver's seat, but Cynthia remained very much aware. The deciphering of things proved a little odd. Her vision wasn't quite the same. The things she found interesting did not grab her wolf's attention at all unless it happened to be a nice pair of leather shoes—mostly because her wolf did enjoy chewing them. But still, a love by them both for fine leather products gave them something in common and a reason to go shopping.

As her wolf, things like scent, the visible evidence of tracks, and other things took precedence. Even better than this different perspective of her situation was the fact that her slimmer paw slid from the manacle with ease. Freedom!

But a freedom to go where, and what shape should she keep? As her wolf, she proved fleet of foot and definitely tougher. Right now, survival trumped her wolf's vanity over their appearance.

Poking her head out the door proved easier than expected, as whoever had left her here didn't latch it all the way. It took a bit of pawing, but she managed to wedge it open, only to find herself in a dark tunnel. The only light came from the bulb in the room. Out here, she noted a hum to the air, a machine-like hum probably from a generator that would explain the electricity to the room.

Lifting her nose, she sniffed. Cement. Dogman. Mold. Somebody else's scent, the same one that she'd vaguely noted in the room with her. Decay also permeated the air, along with something familiar.

Aria?

Her eyes popped open, and she took a step in the direction of Aria's scent. She took another. After a few steps, though, she realized she was going in the opposite direction she'd come from.

I might get lost. She paused, torn between finding her friend and going back for help.

Aria would never turn back. She'd find me. Because Aria was a true gangster with no fear. For her best friend, Cynthia would pretend she was brave, too.

Now just tell that to her racing heart.

On paws that really weren't crazy about the cold and dirty concrete, she tread, passing a few doors, most of them closed and, those that weren't, dark inside. The tunnel had very few lights working, the single bulbs spread few and far between, but at least she could see. Not exactly a good thing in this case.

The farther she went, the more her oh-poop meter waggled and wiggled and begged her to run in the opposite direction. Reminders that Aria needed her, that Cynthia could be brave, bolstered her.

Long gone, though, was the intrepid kidnapper and needle jabber. Things had gotten so dire with the discovery of the body. The adventure Cynthia had boldly gone on had turned sour.

Not entirely sour; we did find Daryl.

And now, even if by accident, she'd found the trail for her friend. The familiar smell teased Cynthia into going on, forcing her to rely on a courage that trembled in fear. Finding a second lone slipper didn't help her shaky confidence.

What if I find her dead body?

Cynthia doubted she could handle that alone. What if she ran in to dogman? She still didn't even have single Scooby Snack. What if she saw a giant rat? There wasn't a single chair to stand on and scream if she did.

The what-ifs piled on top of each other, slowing her pace, until she stood shivering in the dank corridor.

Poop on a stick. What am I doing?

Running off blind again, that was what, and look at how much trouble that got her in most of the time. Perhaps she should do something smart for once, make a mature and informed choice such as going back the way she came and fetching some help.

The dilemma of what to do kept her frozen until she heard the hair-raising howl of something on the hunt. Instinct screamed it came for her.

Eep!

Chapter 22

The shirt Daryl planned to buy for Cyn: *"These tits belong to a jealous boyfriend. Stare at your own risk."*

THE TUNNELS that led from the secret fireplace entrance were long and twisty. They also branched off a few times, but they could have branched off a dozen more. Daryl would have still followed her scent.

His four paws ate the tunnel in giant strides, his feline for once not protesting the fact that it got its feet wet or that they didn't explore the interesting scents permeating the place.

Urgency drove him to run faster and faster, probably

because, from a side tunnel, the fresh scent of the dogman overlay that of Cyn's. It seemed there was more than just one person using these hidden corridors. The lack of steady lighting, and the twists, made it difficult to predict what lay ahead. It didn't help that, in a few spots, parts of the tunnel had caved. While someone had dug an opening through these spots, they proved tight, especially for Constantine, who, being a rather bulky kind of fellow, couldn't always fit his broad shoulders through with ease. As for Princess, she dashed along not daunted at all, her sideways gait and lolling tongue expressing excitement at the chase.

The biggest dilemma came at a fork in the tunnels. Via one, Daryl could scent Cyn, and yet Princess dashed down the other.

"Princess! Come back to Daddy," Constantine called.

But the little dog was off, barking in the distance.

"Shit," Constantine cussed as he loped off after the dog. He shouted, "Dude, I gotta go after Princess, but you should keep going after Cynthia. I'll catch up."

Constantine would have to because Daryl wasn't about to wait for him, not when he heard the echoing howl from the tunnel holding Cyn's scent.

I know that sound. The hunting call of a predator. He put on a burst of speed, pushing himself harder and faster, almost running past an open doorway that suddenly appeared. He slowed his mad dash, but was still caught by surprise by the hairy body that hurtled from the room.

He'd found his recent nemesis—dogman.

Had Daryl worn his human shape, he might have snapped something witty like, "Hey, dog breath, eaten any shit lately?" But cats were more suave than that, so he settled for a *Meowr* and a snarl as they wrestled for dominance.

This time, he kept his panther form rather than resorting to a half-shift. His teeth were sharper this way, his claws more deadly. When the dog thing tackled him to the ground, he paid for it in blood, as Daryl tore the thing's skin to ribbons.

Unlike a normal creature, dogman didn't cry out in pain. He only got madder.

And more slobbery. *Like, ew, wear a fucking bib.*

Then Daryl felt it, an electric sizzle as if someone had touched him with a lightning bolt, except it came from the creature or, more likely, the creature's metal collar.

Daryl released the monster, who hissed and snarled as its fingers grabbed at the ring around its neck.

"You know that won't work, Harold." The man who stepped into view wasn't a stranger to Daryl. While the guy was a few years older, he recognized him as Sheriff Pete's son, Merrill.

The knowledge went a long way and explained why Pete wasn't keen on people finding out what was happening. His son was involved, and not in a good way, judging by the revolver in one hand and the remote in the other.

Given staying a cat wouldn't get him any answers, Daryl swapped shapes and hoped Merrill wouldn't use that moment to shoot him. Bullets hurt. Having gotten shot at a few times when he was younger and liked to play chicken with hunters, Daryl preferred to not explain to his mother, again, why she had to dig bullets out of his flesh.

Stretching to his full height, Daryl eyed the sheriff's son, sparing only a passing glance at the dogman crouched at his feet.

"What are you up to, Merrill?"

"Just doing my job."

"Does doing your job involve killing people and kidnapping others?"

The guy shook his head. "If this is your attempt to get me to talk and spill my guts, then you might as well stop now. I'm not telling you a damned thing. Why bother, when you'll soon be experiencing it? We need new subjects. Your girlfriend will make a good one, but you'll be even better. We don't have any felines to play with."

"I won't be a lab rat for your sick game."

"It's not a game. Everything I have done is fully sanctioned."

"You can't tell me the council agreed to let you kill people."

Merrill's lips twisted. "A regrettable accident. We've had a few recently. But nothing we can't hide. We've been doing it for years. And, now, enough chatter. Get on your knees with your hands behind your back."

"Or what, you'll shoot me? I'd rather die than go willingly with you." Actually, he'd rather chew Merrill's face off and then pee on him, the ultimate feline disdain.

"Who says this gun has bullets?" The smile on the other man's face was anything but reassuring. "The lab prefers its subjects uninjured. Hence why this gun is charged with tranquilizers."

Uh oh. Before Merrill finished talking, Daryl dove to the side, avoiding the first shot. A narrow tunnel, though, didn't give many options for movement. With nothing to lose but his life, Daryl did the only thing he could. He charged Merrill, taking the guy off guard.

They tumbled to the floor, hitting it hard. A metallic clatter let Daryl know Merrill lost his grip on the gun, but he'd kept one on the remote.

"Kill him," Merrill screamed, and Daryl didn't have to hear the low snarl from behind to know dogman—a man who used to be called Harold—rose to the command.

Wrapping his hands around Merrill's throat, he managed one hard tap, two, before instinct had him rolling to the side, and just in time, as Harold pounced.

The impact knocked the remote from Merrill's hand, and Daryl caught a moment of panic flashing in his eyes.

Before he could think on it, Harold jumped on him, hairy paws and claws slashing at him. Daryl caught the fur-covered wrists and held him at bay, barely.

Their struggle pushed him back, the dog-like creature strong, strong enough that Daryl lost ground. His foot stepped on something that crunched. It was enough to make him stumble.

"Fuck. " He grunted the word as he felt himself fall to the floor and then thought it again as he strove to keep Harold from ripping out his throat.

I'm a goner. In that moment, Daryl began mentally

saying goodbye to a few people. His position under Harold definitely placed him at a disadvantage.

The slavering jaws lowered. The wild light in Harold's eyes held not an ounce of humanity, nothing but a killing hunger.

It might have been lights out at that moment if something hadn't hit dogman and knocked him off balance.

Stumbling to his feet, Daryl noted a small wolf facing off against the much bigger Harold.

He could smell the fear radiating from her, see the fright in her eyes, yet she stood there, hackles raised, lip peeled back in a snarl, attempting to defend him.

Ah, how cute.

"Don't you worry, honey. I've got this." Daryl shot the dogman in the back with the tranquilizer gun he'd scooped off the floor. Shot him a second and third time, just to be sure.

Harold snarled, took a staggering step toward Cyn, then slumped to his knees before slamming face-first into the floor. Daryl didn't waste a second longer watching to see if he stayed there. He swung around looking for Merrill, but of the other man, he couldn't find a trace. The bastard had slipped away.

Relief suffused him as he turned back to Cyn and realized she was safe. Safe, yet why did she huddle against the wall, head hanging?

"Are you hurt, honey?" Daryl stepped over Harold and crouched before her. Stretching out his hand, he meant to stroke her, but she swung her head away from him. "What the hell? What's wrong?"

He gave her space as she changed shape, fur getting

absorbed by skin, bones cracking and reshaping. A few blinks of an eye, an agonized moan, and then his mocha honey was slumped before him.

He dragged her into his arms, ignoring her squeak. He squished her in a giant hug. "Fuck me, but I'm glad I found you."

"You came looking for me."

"Well of course I did. You didn't really think I'd let you get kidnapped and not do anything, did you?"

She tilted her head and gave him a small smile. "You're the first man, other than my daddy, to ever rescue me."

"Do you often need rescue?"

She shrugged. "I panic."

"Not this time you didn't. You saved me, Cyn."

She ducked her head. "I couldn't exactly let him eat your face. It's kind of cute."

"Only kind of?" He laughed. "Wait, don't answer that. I'm just glad your wolf came along in time. She's a cutie, by the way."

He felt her stiffen. "You don't have to pretend."

"Pretend what?"

"That there was nothing wrong with my wolf. I've come to grips with it."

"Grips with what?" He frowned. "I didn't see anything wrong with your wolf. Four paws. Fur. Ears. Great big teeth."

"A stubby tail."

He snorted. "And? What of it?"

Her turn to frown. "I don't have a proper wolf tail,

just a little wee stub of one that the doctor says came from my dad."

While it didn't happen often, sometimes inter-breeding of the species mixed up some traits. But Daryl didn't get the big deal. "So what if you've got a bear's ass. I happen to like your ass."

"It doesn't bother you that I'm not perfect?"

Daryl squeezed her tight. "That's where you're wrong, honey. You are perfect. Just the way you are."

"If we weren't in a dark tunnel beside a snoring dog thing, I would so reward you for that remark."

"Don't think we can manage a quickie?"

A shout from up the tunnel. "No, you don't have time. None of us do. We need to find a way out."

Before Daryl could ask why, a rumble shook the tunnel. Then another.

It didn't take a healthy fear of fire for him to realize the smoke he smelled, even if still faint, probably didn't bode well for them.

Constantine appeared, jogging toward them with his little dog tucked under his arm. "Something's happened to the tunnel we came in through. We need to find another way out and fast before the smoke gets any thicker."

"What about him?" Cyn pointed to the slumbering Harold.

Given the trouble dogman had caused, Daryl's first impulse involved leaving him. However, with Merrill having fled, they still needed answers.

"We should bring him."

"I got it." Constantine heaved Harold into a fireman

hold and led the way through the tunnel, but not very far, as another rumble shook the tenuous structure. The flickering light overhead went out, and the next one, yards away, didn't provide much illumination.

Water hit Daryl in the face, a stream of it that got thicker as the ceiling overhead spiderwebbed with cracks, cracks he couldn't really see because of the thick gloom, but could easily imagine.

"Run!" Constantine yelled.

Run where?

They took off sprinting, Daryl holding Cyn's hand tight lest he lose her in their mad and dark dash.

A faint light ahead showed one of the few light bulbs hanging from the ceiling. But more important than that, there was a ladder bolted to the wall nearby it.

Constantine dumped Harold and his dog before he scrabbled up the rusty rungs so he could shove at the trapdoor overhead. It didn't want to move at first. Yet, assaulted by Constantine's determined, shoving shoulder, it creaked, it groaned, and finally inched open. Mud slid into the cracks, but Constantine gritted his teeth and pushed again, heaving past the layer of swamp on top of the hatch to reveal a night sky.

Leaping to the floor, Constantine jerked his head at the opening. "You two go first. Then I'll grab this guy and follow."

With the smoke getting thicker, and an almost visible shiver vibrating the tunnel around them, Daryl wasted no time shoving Cyn at the ladder. He also couldn't help but gaze with a bit too much interest at her bare ass as it wiggled up.

A smart man, Constantine looked the other way. Daryl clung to the rungs next, moving quickly and lithely until he emerged in the swamp. He immediately turned and knelt.

"Hand Harold to me," he told Constantine.

"Princess first."

The little dog didn't seem impressed they were handing her around like a football, but at least she didn't try and tear Daryl's arm off.

Next, Constantine bent down to grab the hairy bastard, but it seemed it wasn't just opossums who could play dead.

With a snarl, Harold leaped and swiped at Constantine. The big man managed to avoid a deadly swipe from those paws, but, in so doing, missed a chance to grab Harold before he bolted away down the hall toward the thick smoke.

Constantine took a step, two, after him, and Daryl barked, "Don't even fucking think about it. This place is about to collapse. He's not worth dying over."

With a sigh, Constantine turned and grabbed the ladder just as another tremor shook the place, a tremor that kept going as something in the distance exploded. Smoke suddenly billowed from the hatch.

Without further ado, Constantine emerged from the ground, yelling, "Move away from it before it collapses."

Eyes wide, Cyn scurried to obey, and with Princess once again scooped off the ground, the three of them ran away, feet sloshing through ankle-deep muck, and didn't stop until they reached a copse of trees with thick trunks. Under its boughs, they huddled as the tunnel they'd just escaped gave a final belch of smoke. The hidden structure collapsed, sucking in a pile of water and muck with it.

The swamp took back what belonged to it, but it hadn't fed on Daryl and his friends, not tonight.

Hopefully not ever.

Chapter 23

Cynthia: *So I think I'm going to stick around Bitten Point.*
Mom: (*silence*)
Cynthia: *Mom?*

IT DIDN'T TAKE AS LONG AS expected to make it back to the B&B, especially since they had a bright beacon to follow in the sky. The hardest part was realizing they'd have to appear naked.

However, that fear proved groundless because Daryl sent Constantine ahead, and the big man snagged them some clothes.

Not much was said during that trek. What could they say? Harold had escaped. The tunnels had collapsed, and the only clues they had to where Aria went were gone. But where? And why?

Questions for the moment that would go unanswered, but other things might come to light. With the murder and the fire at the B&B, this time there was no hiding what happened.

According to the cops who'd witnessed the blaze, the fire seemed to start somewhere under the house. Nobody knew how, but the result lit the sky for hours. And everyone in town knew the place burned.

Everyone who could give a hand fighting the flames showed up, but there was no saving the structure.

Luckily, everyone made it out of the house in time, except for Sheriff Pete. No one had seen him since the inferno began. His men surmised he'd gotten caught in the blaze, but Cynthia—who now had a much closer relationship with sin because of Daryl—figured Sheriff Pete had set it to cover his and Merrill's tracks. Then he'd disappeared, just like Harold, the dog guy, disappeared. She'd like to think they all burned to a crisp, caught by the flames, but even she wasn't that naïve. Evil did like to flourish.

According to the fire chief—and Constantine confirmed—it would be days, if not longer, depending on structure damage, before they could venture into the ruins to look for bodies or to even try and venture into the tunnels leading from the house. The chances of it remaining unscathed, or even navigable, were pegged as unlikely. Whatever the tunnels hid below would stay that way, leaving them with more questions than answers, the biggest question being, was Aria still alive?

It annoyed her that they might never know what had happened. The fire obliterated any clues. Ashes to ashes. Secrets to dust.

From the ruins of disaster, though, rose hope. While Cynthia might not know where Aria was, she wouldn't relinquish the belief that her best friend lived and would find her way. *She's been through too much in her life for it to end so soon.* And Cynthia truly believed her friend was around Bitten Point somewhere, which meant Cynthia would stick around, too. But Aria wasn't the only reason to stay.

I am not going anywhere unless Daryl goes with me.

Since the human world couldn't know of their involvement in the fire at the B&B, it was thought best that Daryl, and Cynthia, vacate the area. Despite the cover-up in their presence, she did have to field one frantic call from her mother.

"Thea, baby girl, thank goodness you're alive. When we heard about the fire, your father went grizzly."

"Tell Dad I'm fine." More than fine, she was going home with Daryl. Home, oddly enough, being wherever Daryl took her.

"Ask your parents what hotel they're at." Daryl didn't turn his head as he asked.

A frown creased her brow. "Why?"

"So I can drop you off. You and your folks should leave town."

"Mom, I'll call you tomorrow." She hung up and stared at him. Poor Daryl seemed tense since they'd left the fire. He clenched the wheel of Constantine's truck that had survived the explosions from the propane tank alongside the house with only a few new dents. His friend said he'd catch a ride with one of his firehouse buddies. Daryl didn't argue, but Cynthia did make a mental note for them to score some wheels. With her car destroyed, and Daryl's on loan to Caleb, they would need transportation. "What's wrong with you?"

"Nothing is wrong with me."

"So why are you trying to dump me on my parents? What happened to hanging out to see where things were going?"

"That was before you almost died. Again!" He slammed his hands off the steering wheel, the jolt sending them swerving before he got control again.

"But I didn't die. Neither did you." And neither did Aria, she hoped. "The only people who have come to an early end are the bad guys. And I say good riddance."

"What if they didn't perish? What if they're still out there?"

She gaped at him as she realized the problem. "You're worried about me."

"Of course I'm fucking worried about you."

"Anyone ever tell you that you're adorable, kitten?" She intentionally teased him.

"Don't call me kitten. Or adorable."

"Why, does it make you think of your mommy?"

She could practically hear the air hissing through his clenched teeth. "This isn't amusing, Cyn."

"If you say so. If you're done whining—"

"I am not whining."

"Says the man who needs a baguette and cheese."

"You're driving me insane, Cyn."

"Good," she retorted as he pulled to a stop by his building. She hopped out of the truck and went skipping up the fire escape. He followed close behind.

This time, nobody waited for them outside or inside. She no sooner entered his apartment than the soot-stained shirt she wore went flying and hit the side of the garbage pail in the kitchen. Close enough.

"Cyn, what are you doing?"

"Getting these smelly things off."

"Then you need to get them right back on because, as soon as I grab some cash, I am putting you on a train back to the city."

"Good luck with that. I am not leaving."

"And I say you are. It's too dangerous for you here."

"It's dangerous for our kind everywhere."

Daryl scrubbed a hand through his hair. "Why must you be so stubborn? I don't want you getting hurt. Dammit. When I realized you were gone..."

Ah, how cute. The big, bad kitty was worried about her. Silly guy. Didn't he understand yet that sending her away wouldn't fix the problem? Perhaps she should point that out.

"So you think putting me on a train, by myself, that will drop me at a huge station downtown, again, by myself, is safer than me staying here with you?"

He blinked. Opened his mouth. Shut it. "There are no murdering dogmen or dinos in the city."

"No, there are crazy taxis and gangs and any number of other bad things that could happen to me. Unless this is your way of saying you don't want me." She thumbed the waistband of her pants and eyed him, wondering if she was misreading things. After all, what sane man would want a girl smelling of smoke and muddy swamp, with hair sticking out in crazy directions?

She wiggled her hips, and while her yoga pants did move down a little, it was on her bare, jiggling breasts his gaze focused.

"I'm getting naked," she said, pushing the fabric over the swell of her buttocks.

"I see that." His fists were clenched tight to his sides, his face even tauter. Yet for all his attempts to appear unaffected, he couldn't hide the heat in his eyes. "Why?"

"Because I'm dirty, Daryl. So very"—shimmer—"very"—shiver—"dirty." Her pants landed in a pool of fabric at her feet, and she stepped out of them. "I'm also very, very much in love with someone."

"You are?"

"Very. And I think he loves me, too, which is why he's so freaked out and trying to send me away."

"If he said yes, would you leave?"

She strode toward him, hips swinging, loving how his gaze locked with hers. She stepped right into him, and he laced his arms around her.

"I'm not leaving you, Daryl. I bit you for a reason. Because you're mine."

With those words, she broke free of his embrace and skipped to the shower. She didn't enter the warm spray alone. Daryl was right behind her.

He spun her under the hot water so he could plaster his lips to hers in a searing kiss. His mouth said what he couldn't. His body spoke the words he didn't know how to say. But she was all right with that because actions were what mattered.

As the water sluiced them clean, wiping the traces of their adventure, she molded herself to him. The heated hardness of his erection pressed against her lower belly, pulsing with excitement. Her sex throbbed as well, arousal already running rampant through her. It took only a touch from Daryl to ignite.

"Take me. I need you," Cynthia gasped in between pants.

"What if I want to go slow?" he murmured in between nibbles of her lower lip. "Maybe I want to take my time for once. Explore every inch of your luscious body. I think I need another taste of your cream. Maybe spend some time sucking those hard little berries of yours."

"Great ideas, for later," she growled. She grabbed his hand and pressed it against her mound. "Right now, I need you take care of this."

A groan left him the moment his fingers touched the slick folds of her sex.

"I want you," she whispered into his mouth.

Those words proved his breaking point. Daryl spun her around until she faced the tile wall. She braced her hands against it as he grabbed at her hips to pull her bottom back.

Without being asked, she spread her feet and tilted her butt to tempt him. The hard head of his cock rubbed against her, spreading the petals of her sex, dipping in enough to wet him with her juices.

He was going slow, so slow. She wiggled her bottom, pushing back and not above begging. "Please."

His hands gripped her waist as he pushed himself deeper. She couldn't help clamping down on him, squeezing his cock tight. It seemed to take forever before he was fully seated inside her, and then he paused.

She might have growled. She definitely pushed back against him, wiggling her bottom to seat him more deeply.

His fingers dug into her hips, and she heard him suck in a breath and then lose control. The withdrawal of his cock was only so he could pump her, slam her, thrust into her willing sex fast and hard. The sound of slapping flesh went well with her moans of pleasure.

Then he stopped.

She made a sound of protest, one he swallowed as he turned her around to face him.

"Put your leg around my waist," he ordered, and grabbed her thigh, bringing it up and, at the same time, exposing her.

He slid back into her, his long cock filling her, his lips finding hers under the warm spray of the shower. Everything was slick and wet.

Faster. Faster. His hips pistoned as he drove into her, each hard slap of his body bringing her pleasure higher. His lips trailed from hers along the line of her jaw, nibbling as he continued to thrust.

As her channel squeezed tighter and tighter, on the cusp of ultimate bliss, his lips feathered across the vulnerable skin of her neck.

Her breathing came in frantic pants. His mouth sucked at her skin. As she let out a low moan of bliss, her body trembled then shuddered as she came and came with violent intensity, as not only his cock spurted hotly within her but his teeth clamped down on her skin to mark her.

Claiming me.

And she couldn't be happier.

Only once they were snuggling in bed awhile later, skin still damp from the shower and flushed from love-making, did she let her fingers trace her newest mark on her neck.

"You bit me again," she stated.

"Yup."

"Why?"

He rolled her on top of him, anchoring her with his hands on the cheeks of her ass. "Because this time I knew what I was doing, and I wanted everyone to see it."

"What are you saying?"

He groaned. "Are you going to make me explain this out loud?"

Her eyes crinkled as she smirked at him. "I am so that there's no mistake."

"Fine. Think of the chomp as my panther claiming you."

"What of the man?"

His lips stretched. "The man wants to live Cyn-fully ever after with you."

What luck, so did she.

Epilogue

Cynthia: *I love him, Dad.*
Dad: *Harrumph. (Translation: I don't think he's good enough for you, so when he hurts you, I will skin him alive.)*
Cynthia: *Love you, too, Daddy.*

WHIR. Scratch. Scratch.

Cynthia awoke to find her mother leaning over her, measuring tape in hand, and a pencil clenched between her teeth.

Used to her mom's weirdness, she didn't make a peep, but Daryl let out a very unmanly "Eep!"

"Don't mind me. Just taking a few measurements." Her mother let the tape suck back into the reel while she jotted down some notes in a binder she'd placed on the nightstand.

Curbing her amusement took Cynthia biting her lips, but she failed to completely muffle a snicker as Daryl made sure the sheet was tucked higher on his chest.

"Measuring what?" he dared ask.

"Uh-oh," Cynthia muttered. "You shouldn't have gone there."

Mom slotted her pencil above an ear and beamed at him. "I am measuring the surface area of the bed and the surrounding floor. I already calculated the swath of space from the front door of your place to the bedroom. I do assume you will be using the front door and not the window again when you bring her back?"

"Bring her back from where? And what exactly do you need all those measurements for?" Daryl straightened to a seated position in bed, his eyes acquiring the wild look she'd noticed more than once in the early images of her dad taken with her mother. Poor Daryl had the look of a big cat caught in crosshairs. No escape.

"It's for the rose petals, of course. I figured we'd have them flutter on the floor in a straight line from the door leading to the bed. Which I've already ordered new linen for. White, of course, so the petals contrast nicely."

"But I like my sheets," Daryl exclaimed, clutching them tighter to his chest.

Her mother sniffed. "Those are bachelor sheets. Once you're married—"

"Married?"

"We'll also look into upgrading your living arrangements. Maybe we'll do it together." It was almost painful to watch the sudden idea bloom, especially since Daryl didn't know any better and had no time to brace. Cynthia bit her inner cheek as Mother dropped her biggest hit yet. "It's time Larry and I relocated somewhere new. I hear there's some nice housing available in town. Perhaps we can find two on the same street or, even better, side by side."

A sane man might have leaped from the bed—naked parts swinging—and run screaming into the bayou. But Cynthia hadn't fallen for Daryl because of his mental stability.

Her bad kitty got a look Cynthia didn't trust, especially since he smiled. No sane man would smile in the face of her mother's machinations. "That all sounds fantastic. We should have you close for when we start popping out kids."

"Kids?" Her mother breathed the word.

"At least a couple. And given you've got the marriage well in hand, I think Cyn and I should get working on that while you scout the local schools."

"Nothing but the best for my grandbabies," her mother crowed as she dashed from the room. "Wait until I tell Luisa we're going to be grandparents."

Cynthia didn't move until she heard the door slam shut. Then she turned on him and exclaimed, "You just told her we're going to have kids. Are you on catnip?"

"No, I'm in love. With you."

And that was all that really mattered.

Life in Bitten Point sucked Cynthia in, and over the next little while, though they didn't find Aria, her friend managed another phone call, a strange one where Aria said, "Don't look for me. I'm fine."

As for Cynthia, she was more than fine. She was in love, and gangster, especially when she got Renny to draw a permanent marker tattoo of a kitten on her butt.

———

STUPID SWAMP. It sucked at her limbs when she tried to rest. It coated her in a slimy second skin that reeked. But at least it hid her from the trackers.

She knew they were out there, searching. Hunting...

Hunting for me so they can drag me back to that place. Never.

She'd been running and hiding for hours, and still, she didn't feel safe.

Knowing what she did, would she ever feel safe again?

An ululating shriek came in the distance, an eerie sound that echoed and froze the breath in her lungs.

They unleashed the hunters. She'd hoped to clear the swamp before that happened. Hell, she'd hoped to make it to a certain safe house before nightfall. However, the bayou hadn't cooperated, and now that nightfall had arrived, the chase was truly on.

As the primal scream came again, she didn't move for a moment, just remained crouched in the mud and weeds, hoping against hope the hunter wouldn't spot her.

For a moment, a shadow appeared against the moon, a rapier-gazed creature aloft on leathery wings.

Did it see her? Would it dive? Would it—

Shrieking in annoyance, it banked and flapped away.

A few dozen heartbeats later, she dared to breathe again and face forward, only to blink at her newest predicament.

Grrr.

The vicious sound came from a beady-eyed creature, muzzle curled back to reveal tiny teeth.

Seriously? She'd eaten squirrels bigger than this for snacks.

But, of more concern was the shadow that rose above them both that said, "Well, well, Princess, what do we have here?"

"Trouble if you don't get out of my way." Aria glared at the big dude through a dirty hank of hair. Even she could admit she lacked an intimidation factor, yet when he dared to laugh, she didn't think twice before acting.

The handful of mud hit the behemoth square in the face with a satisfying splat.

"Did you seriously just do that?" he asked with clear annoyance as he wiped the mud from his face with a hand.

"Get out of my way."

"Or what?"

Perhaps flinging a second handful wasn't the most mature response, but before she could claim he deserved it, Princess attacked.

Be sure to check out the next story, featuring Constantine: Python's Embrace .

Made in the USA
Monee, IL
06 June 2020

32572511R00142